"But you won't go out with me?"

"Jonathan." Gaye seemed to be choosing her words carefully. "I'm not married. I'm not engaged. I'm not involved with anyone. Nor do I dislike you."

"Then..."

"But neither am I in the market for the sort of frivolous, meaningless affair I'm sure you have in mind," she stated firmly. "And despite what you may think to the contrary, I do not mean that insultingly."

"You don't?" Now he was the one having trouble holding back a smile; she certainly had him weighed up. Or, at least, she had, until now.... He couldn't imagine indulging in a meaningless, frivolous affair with her, either. He wasn't sure what he had in mind, but it wouldn't be meaningless!

Jarrett, Jonathan and Jordan
are

Some men are *meant* to marry!

Meet three brothers: Jarrett is the eldest, Hunter by name, hunter by nature. Jonathan's in the middle and a real charmer; there's never been a woman whom he wanted and couldn't have. Jordan is the youngest, and he's devilishly attractive, but he's determined never to succumb to emotional commitment.

These bachelor brothers appear to have it all—looks, wealth, power...but what about love? That's where Abbie, Gaye and Stazy come in.... As Jarrett, Jonathan and Jordan are about to discover—wanting a woman is one thing, winning her heart is quite another!

Look out for Jordan's story!
Coming next month in
To Be a Bridegroom
#2051

CAROLE MORTIMER

To Be a Husband

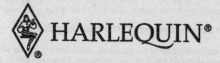

TORONTO • NEW YORK • LONDON
AMSTERDAM • PARIS • SYDNEY • HAMBURG
STOCKHOLM • ATHENS • TOKYO • MILAN • MADRID
PRAGUE • WARSAW • BUDAPEST • AUCKLAND

ISBN 0-373-12043-5

TO BE A HUSBAND

First North American Publication 1999.

Copyright © 1998 by Carole Mortimer.

CHAPTER ONE

GAYE looked up at the man as he walked nonchalantly down the corridor from the security desk toward the nurses' station where she sat. He appeared in no hurry; in fact he strolled along as if he had all the time in the world. Which was unusual in this private maternity home; the men who visited were either new fathers already, or about to become so at any moment. In either case they were usually much more eager to be with their wives or partners at this time than this man appeared to be.

A reluctant father, Gaye decided ruefully. But his casual stroll down the hallway allowed her time to study him even as she waited for the telephone call she had made to be answered. And this man was definitely worth studying—even to Gaye's jaundiced eye...

He was tall, well over six feet, with thick golden-blond hair that was inclined to curl, and a face so perfectly sculptured, he might have been too perfect if it weren't for the fact that at some stage in his life his nose had been broken, leaving it slightly crooked, adding a certain arrogance to his aristocratic face. His dark suit, Gaye could see, no matter how easily he wore it, was tailor-made, and very expensive, the pristine white of the shirt he wore beneath it emphasising his deep mahogany tan.

That tan was even more noticeable as he reached her desk and smiled, his teeth very white and even. 'Hello,' he greeted warmly, laughter-lines crinkling beside the sensuality of his mouth, his gaze appreciative.

Those eyes held Gaye mesmerised as she put her hand over the receiver and looked up at him enquiringly, letting the phone carry on ringing at the other end; it remained unanswered—expectant fathers, despite their wives' obvious condition, could sometimes be most difficult to contact!

But Gaye had never seen eyes the colour of this man's before. A deep, beautiful gold—the colour of gold when it was melted down to liquid, variations of light and dark. Lion's eyes. Amazing!

But as he looked to be in his mid-to-late thirties he was probably well aware of the effect his looks had on women, and Gaye made sure her voice sounded businesslike as she answered him. 'Can I help you?' she enquired.

That devastating smile remained. 'I'm sure you can, Nurse—Royal.' He filled in her surname after a glance at the name-tag pinned to her uniform just above her left breast. 'My name is Hunter, and—'

'Hunter!' she repeated sharply, putting down the telephone receiver to stand up abruptly. 'I was just trying to contact you. We've been telephoning you for the last hour—'

'You have?' He frowned his puzzlement at her sudden urgency on hearing his name. 'But, as I understood the situation, Abbie was only brought in a couple of hours ago—'

'In the early stages of premature labour,' Gaye confirmed, even as she spoke sizing him up for the gown he was shortly going to need. 'Mrs Hunter is on her way to Theatre now. If we hurry, you can still be present for the birth.' As her husband so rightly said, Abbie Hunter had only been admitted two hours ago; her onset of labour was only three weeks early, but there were other complications that had prompted the specialist to decide on an emergency Caesarean; that was the reason they had been trying so desperately to contact her husband. Thank God he had turned up; his wife had been distraught at the thought of him not being with her.

Obviously this man could have no idea of the urgency of his wife's condition, but, even so, from the way he had strolled down the corridor minutes ago, he hadn't been in too much of a hurry to get here, anyway! And his wife was lovely, absolutely beautiful, with a warm personality, and obviously so worried that something was going to go wrong during the birth of the baby she so much wanted.

Gaye's eyes were coolly green as she looked across at the other woman's husband. 'It was my understanding that Mrs Hunter wanted you to be present at the birth.' She quirked blond brows at his obvious reluctance to comply.

He swallowed hard, looking as if he had gone slightly pale beneath his tan. 'She does?'

He was wasting precious time, deliberately so, Gaye felt sure. But it was the patient's welfare that she was concerned with, not his—and Abbie Hunter wanted him with her at their child's birth.

'Come along with me,' she told him briskly. 'I'll see you gowned up, and take you to Theatre myself.' She strode ahead of him down the corridor, tall and loose-limbed, her blue uniform doing little to hide the perfect curves beneath.

Something Mr Hunter was all too aware of, Gaye real-

ised with irritation as she turned back to check he was
following her. Not only was he right behind her, but he
was watching the gentle sway of her hips with obvious
male appreciation! Her opinion of men wasn't very high
at the best of times, but really! This man's wife was in
labour, about to give birth to his child—and he was not
only reluctant to be with her in Theatre, but was ogling
the attributes of another woman. Typical!

Gaye's manner was even more frosty as she provided
them both with Theatre gowns. In all her years of nursing, latterly specialising in midwifery, she had never had
a patient's husband being openly flirtatious with her!

To make matters worse, once they were in Theatre,
he took one look at his wife as she lay sleepily on the
operating table, and went almost the same colour green
as the gown he wore. Wonderful! They were going to
have a faller...!

It happened, of course. Quite a lot of men found it
difficult to cope with normal childbirth, let alone under
these circumstances. But Mr Hunter had seemed such a
self-confident individual, she would never have guessed
he was squeamish. It showed you never could tell...

'Talk to your wife,' Gaye encouraged softly; if he
fainted then the Theatre team would just work around
him where he fell!

He frowned down at her. 'My wife? But—'

'She's sleepy, but awake,' Gaye assured him. 'Talk to
her. It will help.' Both of them, she hoped—Abbie
Hunter to remain calm, her husband to stop from col-
lapsing at their feet!

Pleasure lit up the violet-blue eyes of the woman on
the operating table as she looked up and saw him, although she frowned slightly. 'Jonathan...?'

'Jarrett is on his way, Abbie,' Jonathan reassured her calmly—despite his chalk-white face!—as he stepped forward to her side. 'He'll be with us as soon as he can.'

Well, at least he was doing his bit now, Gaye acknowledged with satisfaction. If they could just stop him from fainting…!

'Just keep talking to her,' Gaye continued to encourage. 'And your son will be with you both very shortly.' It didn't surprise her that this couple knew the sex of their child, or indeed that they had already named him; the Hunter family, like most of the couples who chose to give birth here, were rich and affluent, and it was easier, as regards decorating the nursery and choosing clothes, if they knew the sex of their child before it was born.

Mr Gilchrist had begun the operation now, and it was not the time for a tall, dark-haired man to come striding in, unannounced and ungowned, quickly followed by a protesting midwife. What on earth—?

'Will someone kindly get him out of my Theatre?' the surgeon snarled impatiently as he continued to concentrate on his patient. 'Anyone would think this was a damned circus, not an operating Theatre!' he added disgustedly.

'I'm not about to go anywhere, James,' the tall, dark-haired man informed him imperiously. 'That's *my* wife you have there.' He nodded towards Abbie Hunter. 'And I intend being with her during the birth of our child.'

His wife? *His* child…?

Gaye looked from the dark intruder to the man standing at Abbie Hunter's side, holding her hand; if the newcomer was her husband, then who on earth was *he*?

James Gilchrist was right; this was turning into a circus—and she was in the middle of it!

James Gilchrist straightened, looking frowningly at Abbie Hunter's husband. 'I realise who you are, Jarrett,' he accepted dryly, turning to the man at Abbie's other side. 'And whoever *you* are I suggest you get out and let us get on with the birth of this baby,' he rasped.

The blond man stepped back, taking off his gown and handing it to the dark-haired man who had now come fully into the room. 'With pleasure,' he agreed gratefully. 'I'll be waiting outside,' he told the man called Jarrett—before beating a hasty retreat.

Gaye followed him. Somehow she had made the most terrible gaffe of her career, had taken the wrong man in to see the birth of a baby. But Jonathan Hunter had let her do it! Why on earth hadn't he told her he wasn't Abbie's husband? She was never going to live this down. And as for Mr Gilchrist—!

'Exactly who are you?' Gaye demanded once the two of them were back outside in the corridor, her green eyes flashing like twin jewels.

The colour was slowly coming back into the man's cheeks, the gleam of humour returning into his eyes too. 'Jonathan Hunter,' he supplied unhelpfully, head tilting to one side as she still looked up at him questioningly. 'Uncle, not father, of the baby,' he explained.

Jarrett Hunter's *brother*. Abbie Hunter's *brother-in-law*.

Gaye thought back to the dark man who had stridden so assuredly into the operating Theatre demanding to be at his wife's side, realising now that he had those same unusual golden eyes. But other than that there were no similarities between the two to indicate their relationship, one so tall, dark, and commanding, the other tall and golden-blond, with a lazy ease of charm. Although she had a feeling Jonathan Hunter could be just as arrogant as his brother if the occasion arose...

She looked at him irritatedly. 'Why on earth didn't you tell me that in the beginning?'

He raised mocking blond brows. 'As I recall, you hardly gave me a chance to explain anything!'

Colour suffused her cheeks as she remembered the way she had reacted on hearing his name; as he claimed, she hadn't really given him a chance to explain his relationship to Abbie Hunter. Part of the reason for that, she knew, but would never admit to anyone but herself, was the fact that she had felt the pull of his magnetic attraction from the first. And she had been angry with herself, and him, before he'd even opened his mouth! Her behaviour towards him had been all the sharper because of that.

'If it makes you feel any better,' Jonathan Hunter continued, 'if Jarrett hadn't arrived when he did, he would have expected me to be in there with Abbie.' He nodded in the direction of the operating Theatre they had just left. 'He and Abbie have only been married a couple of years, and this is their first child together. It's unfortunate it happened a little earlier than expected, otherwise I can assure you you would have had no trouble whatsoever contacting Jarrett—because he would already have been at Abbie's side! He only went off to his meeting this morning because Abbie insisted she was fine. But I can also assure you, if he hadn't got here, and I had merely sat outside while Abbie gave birth, Jarrett would have made mincemeat of me!' He grimaced with feeling.

Although he didn't look too bothered at the prospect... Gaye had a feeling very little ruffled his smooth charm. Except...

'Even if it meant you ended up being carried from the operating Theatre unconscious?' she derided.

He grimaced again. 'That wasn't kind, Nurse Royal,' he chided softly.

He hadn't needed to look at her name-tag this time, had obviously remembered her name. Which, for some reason, irritated Gaye too. She was going to have some explaining to do once the Hunter baby was born and Mr Gilchrist had a free moment!

'But true,' she said pointedly.

'It was that obvious?' he muttered self-derisively.

'Let's put it this way,' she teased. 'I don't think green is your colour!'

'But I bet it's yours!' he returned, easily meeting and holding her gaze, open admiration in those golden depths as they looked directly into her eyes.

He was flirting with her again! Okay, so she might now know that he wasn't married to Abbie Hunter, but that didn't mean he wasn't married to someone else. In fact, the chances were that he definitely was attached: his age, his good looks, that charm... He might even have children too. Although, from his behaviour earlier, he definitely hadn't been present at their births!

'I'll show you to the waiting room,' she told him briskly. 'As soon as there is any news, I'm sure your brother will—'

'Uncle Jonathan!' a child's voice called out delightedly. Gaye turned just in time to see an adorable bundle launching herself into Jonathan Hunter's arms. Following close behind her was another tall, good-looking man, with unruly dark hair and devilish golden-coloured eyes.

One more Hunter! This time Gaye was sure of exactly who he was, because where Jarrett and Jonathan, apart from those eyes, managed to look nothing alike, this third man somehow seemed to look like both his brothers.

He also had Jonathan Hunter's way of running an assessing eye over a woman—and the mischievous smile he sent in Gaye's direction, before turning his attention back to his brother and the little girl, told her he had liked what he saw!

'She refused to stay at home,' he explained apologetically to his brother. 'And when Charlie makes up her mind—'

'She can be as doggedly determined as her mother,' Jonathan accepted affectionately. 'And we're all like butter in her hands!'

'Has Mummy had the baby yet?' the little girl asked excitedly—although Gaye hadn't needed to hear her call Abbie Hunter 'Mummy' to know that this was the other woman's daughter from her first marriage; Charlie had the same beauty as her mother—the long dark hair, and the same violet-blue eyes. It was easy to see how this little girl could wind the Hunter men around her little finger; she was *adorable*!

'Not yet, poppet,' Jonathan answered reassuringly. 'But this nice nurse tells me it won't be long now.'

Charlie looked up at Gaye shyly, a dimple appearing in her cheeks as she smiled. 'Is Mummy having the baby now?'

Gaye could feel herself melting as she looked at this

beautiful child. 'She certainly is,' she told her warmly. 'Do you want a brother or sister?'

'Daddy says he wants a little girl who looks just like me,' Charlie told her seriously. 'But I want a brother.'

'Another male for her to charm!' Jonathan groaned, shaking his head.

'Uncle Jonathan says he's going to marry me when I grow up,' Charlie confided guilelessly to Gaye. 'But Daddy says he's too old for me.'

'Far too old,' the newly arrived Hunter agreed mischievously. 'I'm much more your age.'

Charlie shook her head. 'Daddy says you're too old for me too, Uncle Jordan,' she told him regretfully.

Jonathan. Jarrett. And Jordan. Gaye's head was spinning with the three Hunter men. And not just with their names. What a formidable trio they were!

'The waiting room is just down the corridor to your left.' She pointed them in the right direction. 'I'll go and arrange a pot of coffee for you,' she offered. 'What would you like to drink, Charlie?' Her voice noticeably softened as she spoke to the little girl. She had always loved children, and Charlie Hunter was gorgeous!

'A glass of milk, please, Nurse,' the little girl accepted shyly.

'Nurse Royal,' Jonathan Hunter prompted gently.

'You can call me Gaye,' she told Charlie warmly, pointedly omitting to give the two men present the same privilege before going off to the kitchen to get the coffee and milk.

She needed the respite, felt as if her world had suddenly been invaded by a plethora of Hunters. Hopefully, there weren't any more of them. Although, of course, another was just being born. If he was a boy, no doubt his name would begin with a J too—just to add to the confusion!

'Is there anything I can do to help?' offered that smoothly familiar voice Gaye instantly recognised as Jonathan Hunter's. 'Or have I done enough already?' he asked ruefully as he bent down to retrieve the spoon she had just dropped.

Gaye had turned quickly at the sound of his voice, dropping the spoon in her surprise at being interrupted in this way. Jonathan's latter remark had been ambiguous to say the least. Had he done enough already by making her drop the spoon, or had he effectively—or very effectively!—let her make a complete idiot of herself in Theatre earlier?

She looked across at him exasperatedly, receiving a charming smile for her trouble—a smile, she was sure, that usually melted the heart of any female it was directed at. Except that her heart was impenetrable, to Jonathan Hunter's, or indeed any other man's, charm.

'I can manage, thank you,' she returned frostily.

'I'm sure you can. Manage, I mean,' he accepted lightly. 'But I would like to help.'

Gaye looked at his expertly styled hair, his tailor-made suit, the silk shirt, the hand-made shoes—and seriously wondered if he knew one end of a coffee-pot from the other, let alone what you did with it! Somehow, she doubted it. No doubt the Hunter family had servants to do such menial tasks.

'I really can manage,' she told him sharply. 'Would you please go back to the waiting room?' She turned back to the preparation of the coffee, muttering under her breath as she did so. Thank goodness she could go off duty in half an hour. Although the prospect of going home was never a happy one nowadays...

'That was a big sigh...?'

She gave another irritable sigh as she turned back to face Jonathan Hunter. 'I thought you had gone,' she said.

He was leaning back against the door-frame, arms crossed loosely in front of his chest. 'As you can see, I haven't,' he returned unconcernedly. 'I thought, as you won't let me help you, that I could carry the tray through for you when it's ready.'

In other words, he had no intention of leaving! She couldn't say she was altogether surprised; there was a steely determination beneath that charming exterior—even if his step-niece could wrap him around her little finger. Charlie was probably the only female that could...

Gaye couldn't exactly say she had met Jonathan Hunter's type before—he was way out of her league—but nevertheless she felt, for all he was so languidly charming, that there was a much harder side to him. That there was a much harder side to all the Hunter men...

'Why did you sigh just now?' Jonathan lightly interrupted her thoughts.

He also had a doggedness that was fast becoming annoying! Why her? she inwardly groaned. Wasn't her life complicated enough already, without this man's interest? She came to work, she did her job to the best of her ability, she asked nothing of anyone, expected even less, so why had this golden-eyed charmer come into her life at all, with his obvious wealth and boundless charm?

'It's been a long day,' she excused abruptly. And, thankfully, it was nearly over.

He nodded. 'But it must be rewarding. Doing what

you do,' he explained as she frowned across at him. 'Helping to bring life into the world.'

Gaye stared at him. Yes, it was wonderful to see the look of wonder on a new mother's face as her baby was put into her waiting arms. It was the reason she had chosen to specialise in midwifery—because it meant life and not death.

When had she lost sight of that? How had she lost sight of that?

She knew the answer to both those questions. But until this man had questioned her she hadn't realised she had become immune to what she did, to the joy of childbirth; her own life was something she simply got through.

Tears stung her eyes, hot, burning emotion threatening to cascade down her cheeks. She shouldn't cry, mustn't cry, in front of this man. In fact, she couldn't cry in front of anyone. She had held herself firmly in check the last two years; she couldn't start to break down now!

'Gaye...!' Jonathan Hunter was at her side, his hands on her arms, his gaze fixed searchingly on the pale beauty of her face.

It was a face that had grown thinner over the last two years, green eyes appearing huge within its delicately etched contours, cheekbones high, her nose small over generously full lips, her chin and jawline sharply defined, the laughter that had once glowed in the green depths of her eyes too long dampened, adding to her air of vulnerability.

But the last thing she wanted was this man's fleeting concern. She didn't want, or need, his pity. If she ever gave in to the emotions she had kept so firmly in check for so long, then she wasn't sure she would be able to go on at all. When Jonathan Hunter left the clinic today, he wouldn't give her a second thought, whereas her few moments of weakness, of leaning emotionally on someone else, no matter how briefly, would leave her battling to hold up the shaky house of cards that had become her life these last two years.

'Please, Mr Hunter.' She moved away from him, at her chilliest. That coldness had alienated old friends and new acquaintances alike recently—it would keep Jonathan Hunter away too! 'I don't—'

'Jonathan!' Jordan Hunter suddenly appeared in the doorway, his expression jubilant. 'Excuse me butting in, Nurse,' he apologised quickly. 'It's a boy, Jonathan,' he announced excitedly. 'And both he and Abbie are fine,' he added thankfully, obviously as fond of his sister-in-law as Jonathan appeared to be. 'Jarrett has just taken Charlie in to see them both.'

Which had probably also thrilled James Gilchrist! Although from the way Jarrett Hunter had spoken to the consultant earlier, and the way in which he had responded, Jarrett Hunter probably didn't give a damn whether he was thrilled or not!

'That's wonderful news,' Gaye told them both lightly. 'By the time you've drunk your coffee—' she placed the tray in Jonathan Hunter's hands '—your sister-in-law will be in her room, and then you can go and see all of them.' And she would have gone off duty!

'Gaye...?'

She stopped at the door, turning slowly to face Jonathan Hunter, every muscle in her body feeling tense, her nerves stretched to screaming pitch. Why couldn't this man just go back to his life, and leave her to get on with hers?

'Yes?' she prompted stiffly, eyeing him warily.

'Thank you for all your help today,' he told her huskily.

Then he smiled. It was like the sun coming out, his eyes deeply golden, laughter-lines beside his mouth and eyes—even his hair seemed to have taken on a deeper golden glow.

Gaye gave a shake of her head. 'I'm not quite sure what you're thanking me for—almost being present at your nephew's birth or the chance discovery that green isn't your colour!' she replied challengingly. 'I can assure you, it's all in a day's work,' she dismissed before making good her escape.

Because now she had to find Mr Gilchrist, and apologise for turning his theatre into a circus!

Then she had to go home...

Neither was something she particularly looked forward to doing!

CHAPTER TWO

'GREAT legs,' Jordan murmured appreciatively.

'Hmm?' Jonathan rounded frowningly to find his younger brother standing in the corridor beside him, his frown turning to a scowl as he noted the admiration with which Jordan was watching Gaye's departure, obviously enjoying her natural grace of movement as she walked— as he had himself earlier when he'd first arrived at this clinic! As Jordan had pointed out so appreciatively, Gaye had long, shapely legs beneath her uniform.

'Hands—and eyes!—off, little brother,' he warned pointedly. 'And take this to the waiting room on your way back.' He handed the laden tray to Jordan.

'Where are you going?' Jordan demanded to know protestingly.

Gaye didn't just have those wonderful legs to recommend her—her beauty had hit him like a sledgehammer the first time he'd set eyes on her. They certainly hadn't had nurses like her when he was in hospital a few years ago having his appendix out. Which was probably as well—he would never have wanted to recover!

He grinned. 'To talk to a surgeon about a natural mistake,' he said enigmatically, walking away before Jordan asked for an explanation of the remark—knowing his younger brother wouldn't be watching his departure with the same admiration he had Gaye's!

Damn it, but he had been annoyed at Jordan's remark

20

about her legs. Even if it was true! The truth of the matter was, Gaye was gorgeous in every way he could think of. She had a wonderful figure, the fullness of her breasts tapering down to a slender waist, the narrowness of her hips almost coltish when coupled with those long, long legs. And her face! She was so hauntingly beautiful she almost took his breath away, the green depths of her eyes filled with a sadness that brought out every protective instinct he possessed. Beauty and vulnerability—the combination was deadly!

Yet, as he went in search of the specialist who had operated on Abbie, he couldn't help wondering how long Gaye's blond hair would be when it wasn't neatly secured at her nape...

Was she married? If so, then he would swear it wasn't happily! But, happily or not, if she were married, then Jonathan knew he would have to back off. Married women had no appeal for him whatsoever.

He cursed himself now for not paying more attention to her hands, to whether or not she had been wearing a wedding ring. Although he knew not wearing one was no guarantee of anything these days, that some women preferred not to wear a wedding ring any more. Unlike Abbie and Jarrett, who had given each other eternity rings on that day two years ago when they had promised to love each other for ever...

Life, Jonathan decided as he strode purposefully down the corridor, was certainly strange. The three of them—Jonathan and his two brothers—had been conditioned, after a stormy childhood within an unhappy marriage, not to want to take that plunge themselves, and yet he knew for a fact that Jarrett hadn't looked at another woman since he met and married Abbie, and that he never would. How the mighty had fallen!

Now Abbie and Jarrett had a son...

Conor James, he discovered, when he arrived at Abbie's room twenty minutes later. Abbie was still a little groggy, but obviously ecstatically happy. Jarrett was smiling so proudly as he beamed at his wife and son.

As babies went, Jonathan supposed this one was quite pretty—if a boy could be called pretty!—and not at all wrinkled and frowning like every other new-born baby Jonathan had seen. But apart from the fact that Conor was his nephew, that he had his parents' dark hair, and that Jarrett obviously thought he was the most wonderful child ever, Jonathan quickly tired of looking down at the small, defenceless human being, whose only activity seemed to be, from time to time, screwing up his face and stretching out his fingers. Give him a tiny adult like Charlie any day!

Although even she seemed smitten. 'Isn't he gorgeous, Uncle Jonathan?' She glowed up at him from where she sat next to the baby playing with his tiny hands.

'Lovely,' he agreed, wondering how soon he would be able to get away.

Abbie took one look at his face and burst out laughing. 'Wait until it's your own baby, then we'll see how lovely it is!' she teased affectionately, obviously none the worse for Conor's early traumatic birth.

'You'll wait a long time,' Jonathan muttered dryly.

Jarrett gave him a sideways glance. 'Jordan tells us you're smitten,' he taunted, all the time holding tightly on to Abbie's hand.

Jonathan shot his younger brother an impatient glance, receiving only a cheeky grin in return. 'Jordan has a big mouth,' he bit out. 'And now, as all the Hunter board of directors seem to be congregated in this room, perhaps one of us should get back to work and tell the rest of the employees they can go home for the day!'

'Are you volunteering?' Jordan looked at him with innocently wide eyes—eyes that danced with devilment!

'No—*you* are,' Jonathan told him firmly. 'I have something else I have to do.'

'Nurse Royal went off duty ten minutes ago,' Jordan told him with dry mockery.

He glared across the room at his youngest brother. 'How the hell do you know that?'

Jordan gave him a self-satisfied grin. 'I asked,' he answered.

Jonathan's hands clenched at his sides. One of these days he was going to take great pleasure in taking that grin off Jordan's face and ramming it down his—

'We'll see you later, Jonathan,' Jarrett put in lightly, usually the one to act as peacemaker between his two more volatile brothers.

With one last glaring look at Jordan, Jonathan quickly took his leave, promising to return later that evening to visit mother and baby again, hurrying out to the corridor, wondering if he was going to be too late to find Gaye before she left.

He was. There were quite a few people bustling about, some in uniform, others in everyday clothes, but none of them was Gaye. Damn Jordan; if he had been going to ask about Gaye then he should have asked for her address, and not just the time she would be leaving!

It was as he was driving out of the grounds of the

clinic that he spotted her. She was standing across the
road at a bus stop, noticeable to him, in spite of the
dozen or so other people that were also waiting in line.

Jonathan no longer needed to wonder about the length
of her hair; it fell in a thick, straight curtain down to the
middle of her back, her body boyishly slender in a dark
green sweatshirt and pale blue denims. She looked very
young without the officialdom of her uniform, ethereally
lovely.

It took Jonathan some minutes to negotiate the flow
of traffic, all the time hoping the damned bus wouldn't
arrive and whisk her away from under his nose before
he could get the car over to her!

It didn't. Although Gaye seemed totally unaware of
the black BMW parked at the side of the road; those
gorgeous green eyes of hers were staring off into the
distance, but at the same time seeming to see nothing.

It wasn't until Jonathan actually stood directly in front
of her that she became aware of his presence there at
all, and even then she merely looked at him with a complete lack of recognition. Damn it, this woman was de-
stroying his ego!

'Jonathan Hunter,' he reminded her tersely—annoyed
at the necessity of having to do so. 'I thought I could
give you a lift home.'

She blinked long dark lashes as she looked up at him
uncomprehendingly. Then the penny seemed to drop,
and a delicate colour entered her otherwise pale cheeks.
'Mr Hunter,' she acknowledged. 'I—er—the bus is just
coming.' She looked over his shoulder at the approaching vehicle.

Jonathan didn't even turn. 'Then we had better go
now so I can move my car and the bus can pull up.'

'But—'

'Come on, Gaye.' He took a firm hold of her arm and guided her over to the front passenger door of his car, opening it for her to get in. 'We're holding up the traffic,' he told her firmly before closing the door behind her and moving around to his side of the car, putting up an acknowledging hand to the bus driver, then getting in behind the wheel.

Jonathan glanced at Gaye as he switched on the engine, but she sat very still beside him, keeping her gaze straight ahead. He wasn't sure if she was annoyed with him, or just amazed at finding herself seated in his car rather than on the bus. Whatever, he was too busy at the moment getting back into the flow of traffic before the bus driver decided to give him a helping hand by shunting the back of his car. Considering he had only had it a couple of months, he wouldn't be too thrilled if the other man decided to do that!

'Which way?' he asked Gaye once they were finally moving again.

'That's what I was trying to say to you earlier.' She spoke quietly, in that softly melodic voice. 'I live in the suburbs of London, and have a bus and then a train to catch to get home.'

Jonathan shook his head. 'That still doesn't tell me which way.'

She gave him the directions precisely, distinctly, before once again lapsing into silence.

This woman was certainly different, Jonathan decided; he had never met a woman who talked as little as she did. Not that he could stand chattering females either, but this young lady closely resembled a clam! All he knew about her was what he could actually see with his own eyes. She was a trained midwife, tall, blond, green-eyed, probably ten years younger than his own thirty-seven.

But he had known he wanted her from the moment he first looked at her!

Cool, detached, ethereally beautiful—what Jonathan most wanted was to see her naked and wanton in his arms, every vestige of that outer coldness melted away. He had always been ambitious, he acknowledged wryly—if anything, Gaye was more frosty towards him now than she had been earlier!

'You spoke to Mr Gilchrist.'

She spoke so softly, Jonathan wasn't even sure he had heard her correctly. 'Sorry?' he prompted.

'You spoke to Mr Gilchrist earlier.' She spoke more certainly this time. 'In fact,' she went on, 'I think you must have done a little more than talk to him; he actually apologised to me for shouting at me in Theatre in front of everyone!'

Jonathan's mouth quirked at her astonished tone. 'Not in character, hmm?' He had found the specialist bombastic and full of his own importance, but nevertheless he had let it be known that the Hunter family were not impressed by his bullying tactics to a midwife who had, after all, only been trying to do her duty.

He couldn't say he was exactly proud of his own tactics where the other man was concerned, but once again the Hunter name had won through; there had to be some advantages to being one of three brothers who ran one of the most successful corporations in England! Whatever, his conversation with Mr Gilchrist had obviously worked, if he had gone so far as to apologise to Gaye rather than the other way around!

'Not exactly.' She grimaced. 'But I thank you for your intervention, anyway.' There was the ghost of a smile on those wonderfully sensual lips.

Jonathan nodded. 'My pleasure. Would you be feeling grateful enough to have dinner with me this evening?'

Her smile instantly faded. 'Thank you, but no.'

'Just no?' He showed his disappointment; he already had a date for this evening, but he would be happy to break it if it meant he could spend the time with Gaye. 'You aren't even going to think about it?'

'No,' she confirmed flatly.

'Are you married, is that it?' he guessed with a sinking feeling; he could never remember being this intrigued by a woman before. 'If you are, then I'm sorry if I—'

'I'm not married,' Gaye assured him. 'I—I have another commitment this evening.'

The feeling of elation that she wasn't married, after all—his worst fear!—was instantly followed by irritation so strong he had trouble containing it. She was seeing someone else! The thought of her being with another man, smiling at him, laughing with him, kissing him, perhaps doing even more than kissing him, suddenly filled Jonathan with such rage, he had to grip the steering wheel tightly to control it.

What the hell was wrong with him? He was thirty-seven years old, had known many beautiful women in his lifetime, and it had never bothered him before that there had been other men in their lives before him, or, indeed, after him. Yet the thought of some other man laying naked with Gaye made him so angry he could actually have hit something—or someone!

'Break it!' he snarled—and then felt surprised at his

own vehemence. If Gilchrist had acted out of character earlier when he'd apologised to Gaye, then he was acting out of character too now; he was the charming one of the family—he left the arrogance to Jarrett!

Gaye gave him a startled look. 'I beg your pardon?'

'Never mind,' he muttered, shaking his head in self-disgust. 'What about tomorrow evening?'

'I—I'm sorry, but no.' She gave him a pained look.

'The evening after,' he persisted, anticipating her refusal before it was even made. 'Name the evening!' he ground out as she did exactly that.

'Mr Hunter—'

'For God's sake call me Jonathan,' he bit out impatiently. 'You make me sound like your dentist!' Trying to make a date with this woman was proving as difficult as extracting teeth!

She smiled at that, her eyes instantly deeper in colour, like twin emeralds now. 'My dentist is fifty and going bald,' she pointed out.

'So could I be by the time you accept a date with me!' Jonathan countered.

Gaye laughed—and it was the most magical sound Jonathan had ever heard, like delicately tinkling bells. When it stopped, he wanted nothing more but to hear it again. But as she sobered he knew he wasn't going to be that lucky...

'It isn't a policy of your employment or something like that, is it? Not dating the clients,' he explained at her frowning look.

Her mouth quirked ruefully. 'As our clients are all pregnant women, and the men their husbands or partners, it's an unlikely policy,' she returned dryly.

She had a point there! But the alternative was... 'So you just don't like me,' he said harshly.

It didn't happen very often, but it wouldn't be the first time he had been refused a date, either. For goodness' sake, he didn't feel attracted to every woman he met; in fact, he had become very choosy over the last few years. It was just that his attraction to this woman was so strong, he found it difficult to accept that it wasn't reciprocated...

She sighed. 'I didn't say that...'

Somehow this didn't cheer him up! 'But you won't go out with me?'

'Jonathan—' Gaye seemed to be choosing her words carefully '—I'm not married. I'm not engaged. I'm not involved with anyone. Nor do I dislike you.'

'Then—'

'But neither am I in the market for the sort of frivolous, meaningless affair I'm sure you have in mind,' she stated firmly. 'And, despite what you may think to the contrary, I do not mean that insultingly.'

'You don't?' Now he was the one having trouble holding back a smile; she certainly had him weighed up. Or, at least, she had until now... He couldn't imagine indulging in a meaningless, frivolous affair with her, either. He wasn't sure what he had in mind, but it wouldn't be meaningless!

Her smile returned. 'I don't.' She sobered. 'There simply isn't room in my life at the moment for frivolity.'

He frowned at the way she said that, sensing something, but unsure what it was. 'Have you never heard the saying "too much work and not enough play can make Gaye a very dull girl"?' he attempted to tease. 'What do you do in the evenings, every evening, that doesn't leave you time for a social life? Studying for more qualifications? An Open University course? What?'

The harder he probed, the more distant her expression seemed, and the tensing of her body was tangible. He knew he was stepping on ground she considered private, that he was invading it!

'Or maybe it's that you prefer not to eat out?' he continued lightly. 'We could always go to the cinema, or I could try to book tickets for a show—'

'No!' she cut in sharply. 'I've told you, there's no point in my going out with you. Anywhere. At any time,' she added bleakly.

He frowned darkly. 'That sounds pretty final.'

'It is,' she confirmed shortly.

Jonathan didn't like puzzles, and this woman was definitely turning out to be one. She didn't dislike him, but she wouldn't even go out with him, let alone anything else. Perhaps it was the Hunter name itself that put her off...?

'You shouldn't believe everything you read, you know,' he told her.

She turned to give him a startled look, those deep green eyes wide. 'I beg your pardon?'

'The newspapers and gossip-mongers have had a field day with my two brothers and me over the last few years, and since Jarrett married Abbie a couple of years ago the pressure has been placed on Jordan and myself. If we so much as look at a woman the marriage speculation begins,' he explained. 'I just wanted to reassure you that I don't have anyone special in my life already.' The woman he should have been seeing this evening wasn't anyone serious, just someone he spent the occasional night with when they were both free. And went to bed with, he inwardly confessed. But it certainly wasn't serious, its very casualness suiting both parties.

Gaye gave a shrug. 'That's nice to know.'

'But it still makes no difference to your answer,' Jonathan guessed frustratedly. He had never wanted any woman to go out with him as much as he wanted Gaye to. But he knew by her body language that she wasn't going to do so.

'Turn left,' she suddenly instructed at a junction. 'You can drop me off here,' she told him once he had turned the car.

'Here' was the corner of the street, and, although there were several houses close by, if he stopped the car now, they wouldn't actually be parked outside any of them; Gaye didn't even want him to know where she lived, Jonathan realised.

'I'll take you to your door,' he told her grimly. He had never felt so unwanted by a woman in his life. What was wrong with him, for goodness' sake? Because Gaye certainly found something about him unacceptable!

'There's no need—'

'There's every need, damn it,' he told her forcefully. 'I said I would drive you home—and that's exactly what I intend doing!'

He was angry, he suddenly realised. That was an emotion he very rarely felt. But at the moment he was intensely angry. And this woman, with her cool rebuff, was making him feel that way.

Was he really so arrogant that he couldn't take no for an answer?

It wasn't a question of arrogance, he knew; he just couldn't accept that he wouldn't see Gaye again...

'I'm sorry,' he said softly. 'I shouldn't have spoken to you like that. But I still don't have any intention,' he continued determinedly as she would have spoken, 'of just dropping you off in the middle of nowhere!' Or of not knowing exactly where she lived, he decided.

Her green eyes sparkled now as she looked across at him. Jonathan had a feeling anger was as much an alien emotion to Gaye as it was to him. But, he decided, any emotion was better than none!

'The second house on the left,' she bit out, looking away so that he could no longer see her expression.

Although he could guess!

The second house on the left was much further along the road than it sounded, the houses in this quiet suburb obviously exclusive, each set within its own grounds. The buildings themselves, although Victorian in style, were very large and grand. As Jonathan parked the car and looked down the long driveway, he knew Gaye couldn't possibly live in such a large house on her own...

'I—'

'Thank you for the lift home,' she told him politely, the door of the car open even as she spoke.

'Gaye...?' Jonathan moved just as quickly, out of the car, and was standing on the pavement beside her as she got out. 'I don't suppose there's any chance of being invited in for a cup of tea?' he said affably. 'After all, I was almost an expectant father today!'

Her mouth twisted wryly. 'How could I possibly forget?' She grimaced. 'I'll make doubly sure I have the right man in future. I don't want to go dragging some poor unsuspecting male into Theatre to witness the birth of a child!'

He chuckled. 'You should have seen your face when Jarrett walked in!'

'I can imagine.' She groaned her embarrassment. 'Hopefully everyone will have forgotten about it by the time I go back on duty!'

'You won't be at the clinic tomorrow?'

Gaye shook her head, her hair moving silkily about her shoulders. 'I have two days off now.'

Damn! He had thought, had depended on the fact that he would at least be able to see her at the clinic when he visited Abbie. And Gaye had very neatly avoided answering him about the cup of tea!

He gave a frustrated sigh, lightly grasping the tops of her arms. 'You're an infuriating woman, Gaye Royal.'

She gave a rueful quirk of her lips. 'So I've been told—Jonathan Hunter.' She released herself, turning and walking down the gravel driveway to the large, imposing house, without so much as glancing back at him to see if he still watched her.

Somehow Jonathan sensed a reluctance there, felt that this was the last place she wanted to be. Who waited for her behind that huge oak front door?

And who else had told her she was an infuriating woman…? It sounded like something a lover might say. Yet she had told him she didn't have one…

There was so much about Gaye Royal that he either didn't know or didn't understand.

But, whether she liked it or not, he intended finding out!

CHAPTER THREE

JONATHAN HUNTER made Gaye nervous.

Her two days off duty had been more fraught than they usually were, mainly because she had lived in dread of the doorbell ringing, and opening the door to find him standing on the doorstep. He hadn't seemed to her like a man who would accept no for an answer, especially where a woman was concerned. She doubted he had had to very often!

But the doorbell had remained silent. As had the telephone. No one came to the house any more; the telephone calls had ceased long ago. The fickleness of humanity. But, for all his lazy charm, she hadn't received the impression that Jonathan Hunter was a fickle man...

Which made his silence over the last two days doubly nerve-racking! He had been so persistent in trying to get her to go out with him that the silence that had followed her refusal seemed alive with tension.

However, the doorbell hadn't rung, and she hadn't opened the door to find Jonathan Hunter standing there, and by the time she left the house for work this morning she was feeling strangely irritable. It didn't help that the first patient she had to attend to was Abbie Hunter. Or that her arrogant husband was with her.

The other woman was beautiful. Not only that, but she was warm and friendly too. She was also so obviously happy in her marriage. Frankly, Jarrett's aloof manner made Gaye feel as nervous as his brother did, but for different reasons. The golden eyes, which all of the Hunter brothers had, seemed to look at her and see beyond her own cool veneer to the vulnerable woman beneath.

Jarrett Hunter stood up at Gaye's entrance. 'I'll leave you two ladies to chat,' he announced smoothly before bending to kiss his wife and baby son goodbye. 'I'll be back this afternoon,' he told his wife huskily. 'See you later, Gaye,' he said before leaving.

Gaye stared after him; he had known her name! And she could think of only one source...

Abbie laughed softly as she watched her. 'They're very close, these Hunter men. But also very loyal,' she added gently.

Gaye swallowed hard, forcing a bright smile to her lips as she held up the bouquet of flowers she was delivering. 'Roses,' she announced lightly. Although, looking at the room already filled with flowers, it was difficult to know where they were going to go!

Abbie took the flowers, although she made no move to read the card attached to them, still looking up at Gaye. 'Did you enjoy your days off?' she enquired. 'Did you do anything exciting?' she added mischievously.

Gaye thought of those two days off, of the usual routine, the strain of always having to be cheerful. 'No,' she answered flatly.

The other woman raised dark brows. 'No—you didn't enjoy your days off, or no—you didn't do anything exciting?'

No—to both questions! Life had taken a strange turn two years ago, and despite all her efforts she had no idea how to turn it back again. One thing she was certain of:

becoming involved with the Hunter family would only make things more complicated!

'I didn't do anything exciting,' she answered tonelessly.

'Oh.' Abbie looked perplexed. 'Jonathan seemed to think you had a very busy two days ahead of you.'

Jonathan Hunter hadn't thought any such thing. He had been told precisely why she wouldn't go out with him—and it had nothing to do with being too busy!

'Jonathan was mistaken,' Gaye said with a ghost of a smile curving her lips, almost—although not quite—sure this beautiful woman knew exactly what had happened between herself and Jonathan.

'He should be in later today,' Abbie said casually.

Gaye kept her expression deliberately bland, at the same time making a mental note to make sure she was busily ensconced in a store cupboard or something when he arrived. 'That will be nice for you,' she answered noncommittally.

The other woman burst out laughing, a sound of pure enjoyment. 'I'm sorry, Gaye,' she chuckled as she sobered a little. 'It was just that you reminded me of someone else just now. Me,' she supplied at Gaye's questioning look. 'Two years ago, when I was beating an equally hasty retreat from Jarrett's bombardment. And look what happened to me!' She grinned happily, obviously completely content with what had 'happened' to her.

Gaye shook her head. 'The situation is hardly the same,' she dismissed, knowing a little about Abbie's life before she married Jarrett Hunter. She had been a successful model, and then the wife, and widow, of wealthy Daniel Sutherland; apart from the fact that Gaye's parents had been quite well-off, the two of them had very little in common.

What about the Hunter men? crept in a small, betraying voice.

No, not even them, she told herself decidedly. She wanted her life left exactly as it had always been, well out of the limelight, away from the public eye.

'It could be,' Abbie told her softly.

'I don't think so.' Abbie would be discharged in the next day or so, and then Gaye wouldn't have to make a point of making herself scarce when Jonathan Hunter was around... 'I have to get on,' she replied briskly. 'Please ring if there's anything else you want. I'm sure—'

'Next to Jarrett, Jonathan is my favourite man,' Abbie told her huskily.

Gaye turned to her. 'I'm sure he's very nice,' she answered guardedly.

The other woman slowly got up from her chair placed near the window. 'He's more than just nice, Gaye. He—'

'Talking about me again, Abbie?' The youngest Hunter brother bounced into the room, golden eyes alight as he placed a kiss on Abbie's cheek before turning to grin at Gaye. 'Is she telling you how she jilted me in order to marry my big brother?' he said devilishly. 'She promised to be the mother of my children, and then—'

'I promised to be godmother to your children,' his sister-in-law corrected him dryly. 'When you have any, that is! And stop telling Gaye such nonsense, Jordan, or she'll think the whole family is mad!' She shook her head reprovingly.

Not mad, exactly, but they were certainly a family few could ignore. Even if one tried very hard!

'Take my advice and stay well away from Jordan, Gaye,' Abbie told her with an affectionate grin at the man she spoke of. 'He's the breaker of hearts in this family.'

'So it was Jonathan's virtues you were extolling,' Jordan realised mock-disgustedly. 'Gaye, I could tell you a few things about my brother Jonathan that would—'

'Did I hear my name being mentioned in vain?' Jonathan drawled as he strolled into the room, smiling a greeting at Abbie before turning the full force of his gaze onto Gaye.

She could feel the hot colour enter her cheeks as she stared back at him, tall and handsome in the tailored suit and pale blue shirt. When Abbie had said Jonathan would be in later, she hadn't realised the other woman meant almost immediately! But by the too innocent expression on Abbie's face as Gaye glanced at her Gaye realised she had known only too well that Jonathan's arrival was imminent. Was that the reason she had kept Gaye talking…?

This family wasn't just unforgettable; they were also dangerous. All of them!

'I shouldn't listen to anything Jordan has to say, on any subject, if I were you, Gaye,' Jonathan told her merrily. 'It's inevitably suspect.'

'That's all the thanks I get for delaying Gaye's departure until you had parked the car,' Jordan muttered, his irritated tone belied by the mischievous twinkle in his eyes.

A family conspiracy! Gaye had thought she might have been being fanciful where Abbie Hunter was concerned, but as the other woman gave her an apologetic smile she knew her first suspicion had been correct. This family certainly wasn't mad!

Just what had Jonathan told them about her for them all to be behaving this way...?

'Remind me to thank you for that later, Jordan,' Jonathan rasped, giving his brother a narrow-eyed look of warning before turning back to Gaye. 'Have you had a good two days off?' His tone softened as he spoke to her.

'Busy,' she bit out abruptly, challengingly; after all, wasn't that what he had told his relatives?

She felt sure that, under normal circumstances, Jonathan's family wouldn't even have been aware of her existence; she would just have been a woman he'd asked to go out with him and had turned him down. She was sure his family didn't usually get to hear about his rejections! Or, perhaps, it had never happened before...?

Men like Jonathan Hunter were rare, she acknowledged: handsome, charming, self-confident, incredibly rich, and, best of all, still single. Most women wouldn't have turned down an invitation from him! But she had her reasons, very good ones, and no amount of cajoling from either Jonathan or his family would change her mind.

Although, she had to admit, being around the Hunter family certainly kept one on one's toes!

'It gets easier,' Abbie assured her gently, seeming to sense Gaye's mental turmoil.

Gaye had no intention of staying around long enough to find out! 'For your sake, I sincerely hope so,' she returned with feeling. Thank goodness, for her own sake, Abbie Hunter would be discharged from the clinic soon.

'I'll leave you now to talk with your two visitors,' Gaye added, keeping her gaze firmly averted from Jonathan as she knew he continued to watch her with those enigmatic golden eyes.

He did make her nervous. There was about him the same air of self-confident stillness she had sensed earlier in Jarrett Hunter, a quiet determination that ensured he arrived at wherever it was he wanted to go. As she looked at him now, the forceful glint in his eyes seemed to imply that the silence of the last two days had merely been a pause, not an end, in his pursuit—

She was being fanciful now. He had asked her out, she had refused; that was the end of his pursuit. There were too many women out there willing to say yes for Jonathan Hunter to bother with the ones who said no.

She felt a heavy weight settle inside her, and knew it was the responsibility she carried around with her. Always...

'Try not to tire yourself out,' she advised Abbie before turning sharply on her heels and leaving the room, aware that she was once again very close to tears. What was it about Jonathan Hunter that affected her in this way?

What on earth was wrong with her? she chastised herself later as she accompanied Mr Gilchrist on his round. But she knew the answer to that all too well. She had chosen a life for herself in the last two years, a life that was necessarily apart from friendships of any kind, and Jonathan Hunter and his family, with their witty dialogues and underlying kindness, broke through that defence, showing her all too vividly glimpses of what she was missing. Just those brief glimpses made her yearn for something she couldn't have: friends, stimulating conversation, a social life that at times could become too hectic. All gone now. And in its place was loneliness, silence, pretence—and the latter was something she had, ironically, never been good at!

She drank her morning coffee alone in the canteen. Through choice. She had only worked at the clinic for six months, but she had already learnt during that time that making friends with any of the other midwives meant familiarity, and familiarity encouraged questions, questions she had no intention of answering. So she kept herself aloof. And alone…

'Mind if I join you?'

She looked up sharply at the familiar sound of that voice.

'Jonathan…!' She recognised him instantly, looking about them uncomfortably, noticing several curious glances being cast their way by other members of staff also taking their coffee-breaks, the female glances openly admiring as they looked at Jonathan.

Most of the staff were aware that Abbie Hunter was staying in the clinic, and they possibly also recognised Jonathan as having visited his sister-in-law during the last two days. His presence here now wasn't going to comply with Gaye's wish for a quiet, unobtrusive life at all!

'I'm afraid you've come into the wrong room, Mr Hunter.' She deliberately made her voice slightly louder than normal. 'The visitors' tea room is—'

'But I don't want the visitors' tea room,' he cut in smoothly, uncaring of the interest they were engaging. 'I want to have coffee with you,' he announced determinedly as he sat down in the chair opposite hers at the table.

Gaye closed her eyes, groaning softly, only to find

Jonathan looking across at her with calm query when she opened them again. 'Not here,' she told him with soft intensity, willing him to get up and leave.

Which he didn't, of course, do! This man, she decided, had a habit of being in the wrong place at the wrong time—and he had the ability to take her with him!

'Why not?' He looked about the room curiously, a large, well-lit room, its windows facing out over the clinic gardens. 'It seems very pleasant in here.' He turned back to Gaye, looking down into her cup. 'The coffee looks good too.'

'It is,' she confirmed impatiently. 'But you aren't supposed to be in here. And you're drawing attention to the two of us,' she told him more forcefully.

Jonathan tilted his head as he gave her a considering glance. 'And you don't like that, do you?' he said slowly, obviously completely unconcerned himself at the attention his extreme good looks were drawing in their direction. 'They're only curious, Gaye.' He shrugged dismissively. 'It isn't important.'

'It is to me,' she insisted. 'I don't like being the subject of gossip and speculation.' She shuddered at the thought of it.

There had already been enough of that over the last two years without it all starting up again. Anonymity was the reason she lived the way that she did; she had no intention of having that taken away because of this man's determination to make a nuisance of himself!

Jonathan gave a smile. 'I've got news for you, Gaye: there is no way on earth you will ever stop people gossiping or speculating about you, or anybody else! I learnt that years ago, and I've learnt not to let it bother me.'

'Well, it bothers me!' She pushed away her half-drunk

cup of coffee before standing up. 'I think I'll go back to work now.'

It was only once she was outside in the corridor, and found Jonathan at her side, that she realised he must have followed her from the room. She was tall herself, but he towered well over her, and the broad width of his shoulders in his fitted suit seemed to offer a protection she so badly needed— No! She didn't need anyone, least of all a man like Jonathan Hunter, a man who, in his own words, had the newspapers and gossip-mongers following his every move. She didn't want any part of that!

'Shouldn't you be getting back to work too?' she said pointedly as he made no move to leave her side.

He gave that slow, lazy smile that caused an instant fluttering sensation in her chest. 'One of the advantages of being a part-owner of a company: I'm answerable only to myself concerning the amount of time I put in at the office.'

Which meant he could hang around here all day being a pest if he chose to do so!

'Well, some of us aren't that lucky,' she told him bluntly as she stopped outside her ward. 'Goodbye again, Mr Hun—'

'It was Jonathan earlier,' he reminded her gruffly as he put a lightly restraining hand on her arm, letting her know he had noticed that slip in her defences earlier. 'Gaye, there are some things I want to talk to you about—'

'What things?' She had become suddenly still, her expression apprehension as she stared up at him with wide green eyes.

Jonathan looked down at her with concern. 'Gaye— You're right,' he said as two junior midwives went past them in the corridor, giggling and talking softly together, obviously about the two of them. 'This isn't the place for this. I'll pick you up here when you finish work, and we can go for a drink somewhere and talk—'

'No! I mean— No.' She forced herself to remain calm. 'I—have things to do straight after work. I— Perhaps I could meet you later,' she went on agitatedly, not really wanting to meet him at all, but conscious of those things he might want to talk to her about. Maybe this was the reason he had been so quiet the last two days; he had been patiently biding his time, knew he only had to say the right words to get her to agree to meet him, after all. Abbie Hunter was wrong; this man wasn't nice at all! 'There's a pub just around the corner from my home. The Swan. I'll meet you there at nine-thirty,' she told him brusquely, moving away from his restraining hand as she turned to leave.

'Gaye…?' Jonathan called softly after her down the corridor.

She drew in a deep breath before turning reluctantly to face him. 'Yes?' she sighed.

He smiled again. 'If I arrive first, what shall I order you to drink?'

She couldn't respond to the gentle teasing in his voice, or that smile that had affected her so much seconds earlier; she was too tense, too worried to be able to relax. What things did he want to talk to her about? What did he know?

'If you think you know so much about me, then I suggest you guess!' she bit out tautly, this time leaving without hindrance.

But she couldn't resist a glance back before going through the double doors of the ward, startled as she found Jonathan still standing exactly where she had left him, a perplexed expression on his face as he returned her gaze. Why should he be the one feeling perplexed? He wasn't the one on the defensive!

'Nine-thirty,' he confirmed.

Gaye gave him one last frowning look before hurrying back to work. She had thought he was trouble the first time she'd looked at him—and he had done nothing since that time to disabuse her of her belief!

CHAPTER FOUR

WHAT things was Jonathan going to find to talk to Gaye about?

He had arrived at The Swan shortly before nine-thirty, had bought a whisky for himself, and a glass of white wine for Gaye—because she looked more like a white wine drinker than beer!—and now he was left sitting on tenterhooks at a corner table of the rapidly filling public house, desperately searching his brain for something important enough to talk to her about that warranted the two of them meeting like this!

Because there was absolutely nothing he could think of! He had come out with his statement initially in sheer desperation because he couldn't think of any other way to stop her just walking away from him, ever conscious of the fact that Abbie and Conor were due to be discharged at any time; with that his reason to visit the clinic, and see Gaye, would be gone...

But now he was left with the problem of what to talk to Gaye about! She wasn't going to be too happy with him if—

She had arrived!

He had been keeping a surreptitious eye on the door, while at the same time trying to look as if he wasn't really waiting for anyone, despite the obviousness of the glass of white wine. Because a part of him hadn't been sure Gaye would turn up... And he could imagine nothing worse than having to get up and leave, with everyone else in the room aware he had been stood up. Not that it had ever happened to him before, but with Gaye he had already learnt to expect the unexpected.

Like this evening. She seemed different again. Because he knew, if she was here at all, it was under protest, and he hadn't really known what to expect of her. Of course the uniform was gone, but so were the jeans and sweatshirt he had seen her in a couple of days ago, and in their place was a green silk blouse tucked into a pencil-slim black skirt, her legs long and shapely beneath its short length, the heels on her neat black shoes adding to her height. She looked gorgeous! Something, Jonathan noticed with a scowl, that every other man in the room appreciated.

Those male heads continued to turn as she crossed the room to join him, golden-blonde hair loose down her back, an enigmatic smile on those full, sensuous lips, green eyes bright and glowing.

She was beautiful, Jonathan acknowledged for the dozenth time. It still seemed incredible to him that she wasn't already married, or otherwise involved. But she claimed she wasn't, and he had no reason to doubt her. Except for the slightly uneasy feeling he had that she was keeping something from him, a feeling added to by the fact that she was so determined to keep him away from her home. She had done it again this evening, arranging to meet him here so that he didn't call for her. That, he admitted, he didn't like. But for the moment just seeing her was enough. It would have to be!

He stood up as she reached the table. 'I'm glad you could make it,' he told her warmly.

She looked at him from beneath lowered lashes as she sat down. 'I said I would be here.' She spoke in those husky tones that he found so arousing. 'Did you think I wouldn't?'

He hadn't been sure, he admitted to himself now. Her sudden acquiescence earlier could just have been her way of getting rid of him. Although, if she hadn't turned up, there was always the danger of him arriving at the home she was at such pains to keep him away from...!

He smiled as he sat down next to her. 'I got you a white wine; I hope that's okay?'

She smelt heavenly, nothing too heavy or floral, but a perfume as uniquely beautiful as the woman herself.

She took a sip of the wine, relaxing back in the chair as she did so. 'It's fine, thank you. I'm glad to see it's still nice in here; I wondered, after I had suggested it, if it had changed.' She looked about them appreciatively.

It was one of those up-market pubs that seemed to be flourishing at the moment—plush carpets, comfortable chairs, wallpaper on the walls, no busty barmaid behind the bar but a plump, motherly looking woman and a middle-aged man who looked as if he might be her husband.

But Jonathan had little interest in their surroundings. 'How long is it since you were last in here?' Despite the fact that he had voiced the question casually, Gaye gave him a sharp look before replying.

'A while,' she said noncommittally.

Very helpful! 'I just thought that, as it is effectively your local—'

'I rarely go into public houses,' she told him abruptly.

That put him firmly in his place! 'Believe it or not,' he returned dryly, 'neither do I!'

Gaye turned to give him a considering look, her gaze extremely direct as she took in his appearance—the pale lemon shirt, brown jacket, and beige trousers. 'I believe you,' she finally answered.

Now he felt overdressed! But this was as casual as it got; he drew the line at wearing jeans, as the majority of men in the room were doing. Warm, and uncomfortable, they always managed to look creased and well-worn too.

Gaye was still watching him, and suddenly she laughed, that light, melodic sound he had heard from her only once before. It was worth waiting for! The sound itself was magical, but her eyes also became greener, her face alight with what looked like almost childish pleasure. He found the effect so enchanting that he didn't even mind that it was him she was obviously laughing at!

'You look fine as you are,' she assured him, taking another sip of her wine. 'And this wine is just the way I like it—cool and dry.'

'Careful, Gaye,' he drawled. 'If you're too nice to me, I might take that as a sign of encouragement.'

She gave a mocking shake of her head. 'I believe you're far too intelligent to think that!'

Jonathan shrugged. 'I believe intelligence goes out the window when a man is with a woman whom he finds attractive.'

Gaye didn't actually move away, not physically, and yet Jonathan could sense her inner withdrawal from him. Damn. The evening hadn't been in the least tense until that moment; what an idiot he was! This woman wasn't like any other woman he had dated over the years, didn't respond to flirting—or, in fact, the truth!

'See what I mean!' he said with mock self-disgust. 'Stupid, or what?'

To his relief, she actually laughed again. 'I doubt it happens to you very often,' she responded teasingly.

Around this woman, all too often! Jordan, for one, would have been amazed at his lack of finesse where Gaye was concerned. He was supposed to be the charmingly persuasive one of the family—so much for charm now! He had more chance of succeeding with her when he made an idiot of himself!

'More often and more recently than you might realise,' he said dryly.

'Oh, I don't know.' She raised sceptical brows. 'I think allowing yourself to be taken into Theatre for the birth of your future nephew ranks up there with—'

'Okay, okay.' He held up his hand, grinning at her. 'Let's call it quits on that one, and start again.' He held out his hand. 'Hi, I'm Jonathan Hunter.' He introduced himself lightly.

After a short hesitation she briefly shook his proffered hand. 'Gaye Royal,' she supplied shyly.

Jonathan nodded. 'It's an unusual name.'

She looked at him piercingly, and once again Jonathan could sense her inner withdrawal. So much for starting again! The trouble was, he didn't know what to do or say to her, didn't know where the minefields were.

'Royal?' she said sharply. 'I don't think—'

'No—Gaye,' he corrected her instantly, knowing as he could feel the tension leave her that it had been the right thing to say.

It was becoming more and more obvious, as he got to know her, that Gaye had something to hide. And she was determined he wouldn't find out what it was. Ordinarily he would have respected her wish for privacy. But it was that very privacy which was keeping him from getting closer to her, acting as a barrier he couldn't get by, past, or through.

Lazy charm had got him where he wanted to go most of his life, but that didn't mean he didn't also have his own share of the Hunter determination. Because he most certainly did. Where Gaye was concerned, it had kicked into overdrive!

'Do you have any brothers or sisters, Gaye?' he continued conversationally.

'No,' she bit out. 'Why?' Her gaze was openly direct.

'No reason.' He shrugged. 'Just taking an interest.'

'I would rather you didn't,' she snapped. 'You asked to meet me so that you could discuss something with me,' she reminded him coolly.

He had known this had to come, was surprised it had taken this long. He was pleased, he had to admit. At least he had been able to hear her laugh again, spend some time with her, before she got up and walked out on him!

He inhaled deeply. 'The thing is, Gaye—'

'Gaye!' A hearty male voice broke in on their conversation. 'It *is* you, isn't it, Gaye?' The man came to an expectant halt in front of their table.

Jonathan looked up at him with narrowed eyes, grateful for the interruption. But as he took in the good-looking man with unruly dark hair and laughing blue eyes—eyes that looked at Gaye with open pleasure—he wasn't sure he was going to continue feeling that way! There was also something vaguely familiar about the raffishly attractive stranger. Jonathan felt as if he should know him. Yet he knew he had never met the man before. He would have remembered someone this charismatic. However, that feeling of familiarity continued...

Then he became aware of Gaye's continued silence, but as he turned to look at her he could see the reason for it. She looked absolutely stricken, her eyes hauntingly green now in her otherwise pale face. This man, whoever he was, was not someone Gaye was pleased to see.

The man began to look uncomfortable as both Gaye and Jonathan looked up at him without speaking. 'My mistake,' he finally said. 'Sorry.' He grinned at Gaye. 'I must have you confused with someone else. It's been a while—people change,' he added, although his gaze remained fixed on Gaye.

Because he knew, as both Jonathan and Gaye knew too, that he hadn't made a mistake. But Gaye continued to look at him coldly, and it became obvious she wasn't going to admit he hadn't made a mistake, after all.

'Sorry I interrupted your evening,' the man drawled before going off to rejoin his group of friends who stood at the bar.

He left a tense silence behind him, Gaye sitting unmoving beside Jonathan now, so tense she looked as if she might break if he attempted to touch her. Once again, he was grateful for having been let off explaining why he wanted to see her tonight, but at the same time he could have wished he had been prevented from answering some other way.

'Shall I take you out of here?' Jonathan offered softly.

She blinked, focusing on him with effort—almost as if she had forgotten he was sitting at her side. 'What?' Her voice was agitated.

Jonathan couldn't stop himself any longer; he had to reach out to her, his hand light on her arm, although for a brief moment he felt her flinch away from even so impersonal a contact. Then she relaxed, her breath leaving her in a shaky sigh, turning visibly away from the group of people crowded noisily around the bar.

Away from the man who had spoken to her... He was still glancing in their direction, a satisfied smile quirking his lips as his gaze rested on Gaye, as if he knew he hadn't made a mistake!

'Would you like to leave?' Jonathan asked Gaye once again, instinctively knowing the other man's interruption had put an end to their evening.

Gaye had been totally thrown by the encounter, was obviously deeply disturbed. And Jonathan didn't want her disturbed, much preferred it when she teased and laughed. Although he accepted that wasn't likely to happen again this evening.

'Yes—I would like to leave,' Gaye finally answered him stiltedly, her hand shaking slightly as she put down the glass of wine she had been clutching to her the last few minutes. 'Now,' she added with a shudder, keeping her eyes averted from the direction of the bar. More importantly, from the tall good-looking man who had spoken to them...

Jonathan's hand rested protectively on her spine as they made their way to the door, and he could feel the tension in her back, knew that she was holding herself under tight control. He already knew her well enough to realise she would be furious with herself if she lost that control before they got outside.

She drew in deep breaths of air once they were outside, while at the same time avoiding looking at Jonathan.

'My car is just over here,' he told her quietly, walking the short distance to his vehicle and unlocking the door.

Gaye got into the passenger seat without protest, although, once inside, she just sat woodenly, staring straight ahead in the semi-darkness.

Jonathan closed the door softly behind her before moving round to the driver's side and getting in beside her. He made no effort to start the car engine, unsure of what Gaye wanted him to do.

Unsure, too, of what he wanted to do!

He was attracted to Gaye, and part of that attraction, he freely admitted, was that air of elusive mystery she carried around with her. But, by the same token, his relationships to date had been without complications, carefree affairs that didn't put too much strain on his emotions. If he became any deeper involved with Gaye he knew that wasn't going to be the case...

He turned to her sharply as he heard her give a shuddering gasp, and in the rapidly fading light he could see the fall of tears on her cheeks, the faint quiver of her body as she tried to contain herself—and failed.

It was too late for him to back off, Jonathan realised in that moment; he already cared too much; the sight of Gaye crying was almost too much to bear.

'Gaye!' He reached out and pulled her effortlessly into his arms, holding her there even when she would have pulled away, that initial resistance all that she gave as she finally succumbed to deep, heart-wrenching tears.

She wept in his arms until it seemed she had no more tears left inside her to cry, finally moving back slightly to give an embarrassed smile. 'I've made your shirt all wet,' she pointed out shakily.

'It will soon dry,' he soothed, still slightly shaken himself by the realisation that he more than just wanted this woman.

Gaye looked up at him, her head tilted to one side. 'Is it always that easy for you?' she asked. 'Fix it? Or if it isn't fixable just throw it away and replace it?' she explained at his questioning look.

'It's only a shirt, Gaye,' he dismissed—although he knew only too well that wasn't what she had meant at all. That was usually his way, yes; if something didn't work, or it was too much effort, then he got it out of his life.

It was the way he had dealt with all his relationships in the past...

But for the moment his gaze was fixed on the vulnerability of Gaye's mouth. A mouth bare of lip-gloss. That was probably on his shirt-front too! But, with or without lip-gloss, her mouth was so inviting. Too inviting!

He firmly pushed to the back of his mind his uneasiness at becoming involved with this woman. He wanted to kiss her.

And kiss her he did...

Whether she had expected it or not, she didn't resist. And that lack of resistance was all the encouragement Jonathan needed. If he needed any at all!

She felt as light as gossamer in his arms, her lips trembling slightly against his initially, but then she seemed as lost in the wonder of their kiss as he was, her arms curved about his neck, her mouth moving erotically against his, open to his more intimate caress, his hand entangled in the thick golden hair at her nape as he held her to him.

Unbelievable. Mindless. There was only Gaye. The feel of her. The smell of her. The touch of her fingers as they became entwined in the thickness of his hair resting on his collar.

How long he went on sipping the nectar from her lips, feeling the press of her breasts against his chest, the restless roaming of her hands on his back, he had no idea. He was simply lost in the mind-drugging scent and feel of her.

It was dark outside the car when Jonathan finally lifted his head, the only illumination now coming from the overhead lights of the car park; Gaye's face was in shadow, only her hair continuing to glow like gold, her breathing a mere shallow gasp compared with the laboured sounds that came from his own throat.

'Take me home with you.'

Jonathan's breathing seemed to stop altogether as her words sank through the fog that had enveloped his brain. Take her home with him...? 'Gaye...?'

'No! Forget I said that!' she hastily dismissed, pulling away from him, covering her face with her hands. 'I don't know—I wasn't—'

'Who was that man in there, Gaye?' Jonathan rasped, reaching out to grasp her wrists and take her hands away from her face.

She looked up at him with widely startled eyes, their greenness almost luminous in the light given off outside. 'I—' She moistened dry lips. 'I don't know what you're talking about.' The coolness was back in her voice, the need to distance herself.

Especially from Jonathan!

But it was too late for that. She knew exactly what he was talking about; she just didn't want to answer him.

'The man a few moments ago,' Jonathan persisted. 'He obviously knew you—'

'I—'

'And you obviously knew him,' Jonathan concluded, his gaze steadily meeting hers. That wasn't easy to do; those green eyes looked full of pain. A pain she wasn't going to talk about...?

'He isn't important,' Gaye told him stubbornly.

'I happen to think he is,' Jonathan answered just as firmly.

'I'm not responsible for what you choose to think, Jonathan,' she said stiltedly. 'It was obviously a mistake to meet you at all this evening. I only did so because you told me you had something you needed to talk to me about,' she went on accusingly. 'But you obviously didn't—'

'I do now,' Jonathan cut in harshly. 'And if you don't tell me who that man is, Gaye, then I'll have no choice but to walk back into the pub and damn well ask him!' This was too important, he felt, to be simply pushed to one side and forgotten. That chance meeting had prompted Gaye to ask to go home with him, for goodness' sake!

From the accusing glitter of Gaye's eyes, she knew he meant exactly what he said!

She shook her head. 'You have no right—'

'You gave me that right a few minutes ago when you asked to come home with me,' he responded.

She drew in a ragged breath. 'That was a mistake—'

'Some mistakes can't be undone.' He refused to back off from this, was sure the other man was relevant—no matter what Gaye might try to claim to the contrary.

Her eyes flashed angrily. 'You have no place in my life,' she stated flatly. 'Therefore, I have no intention of answering your questions—'

'Again, what happened between us a few minutes ago gives me that right.' Jonathan refused to be diverted.

Gaye's mouth twisted slightly. 'I find it very hard to believe you take this much interest in the lives of all the women you've kissed!' She knew she was being deliberately insulting.

Jonathan knew it too! 'I know exactly what you're trying to do, Gaye—and it isn't going to work,' he grated. 'You're dealing here with the champion of diversive tactics. Where business is concerned, I hasten to add,' he put in at her knowing look. 'I can divert, Gaye, but I'm very rarely diverted from a course myself,' he warned.

She gave a weary sigh. 'What possible purpose will it serve for you to know about Richard?'

'Richard? Is that his name?' Jonathan frowned thoughtfully. 'Hell, yes—of course it is!' He slapped the steering-wheel impatiently. 'I wondered why he looked so familiar. He's Richard Craven, isn't he? The actor.' He knew the other man now, had seen him rise from television star to international film star. And he knew Gaye.

More to the point, Gaye knew him...

She swallowed hard. 'Yes,' she confirmed abruptly. 'I simply can't believe that the first time in months that I actually go out I have to accidentally bump into him!' She shuddered.

'Life is a series of accidental meetings,' Jonathan muttered, still occupied with thoughts of Gaye knowing Richard Craven; it had recently been rumoured in the newspapers that he would shortly be moving to Hollywood. Jonathan couldn't help but wish, in the circumstances, that the other man had already gone!

'As our own was,' Gaye put in quietly.

'Exactly,' Jonathan nodded. 'So how is it that you're acquainted with Richard Craven?'

She gave a humourless smile. 'Does it seem so incredible that I could know such a man?'

'Not incredible, no.' An obstacle he didn't need, was what it seemed! He was also curious as to how Gaye and Richard Craven could possibly have met at all, considering the differences in their careers. As far as he was aware, Richard Craven didn't have any children, so the possibility of meeting through the clinic appeared to be a non-starter. Although it could explain Gaye's reluctance to go out with another man—himself!—because she had met *him* at the clinic…?

'I don't know him, Jonathan,' Gaye finally answered. 'I knew him.'

'The context is unimportant—'

'Not to me it isn't,' she interrupted forcefully. 'Richard and I— Two years ago we were engaged to be married!'

Jonathan stared at her. Gaye—and Richard Craven…? Aloof and elusive Gaye, and that too handsome man, whose star was rapidly ascending, didn't just know each other as past acquaintances; they had been engaged to be married!

A stream of questions hurtled haphazardly into Jonathan's brain, falling over themselves in a need to be asked…

CHAPTER FIVE

GAYE sat with her eyes firmly closed, her hands clenched at her sides. She wouldn't cry. Not again. Because it would look as if she was crying for Richard. And she wouldn't be. She had got over his betrayal a long time ago.

She wanted to cry for something else completely.

But her sorrow was spent now. Had been long overdue. She suddenly felt lighter for the release, somehow, she realised, more able to bear the responsibility that had been hers for so long.

She turned to smile at Jonathan, that smile fading as she saw the harsh anger in his face, bringing her back to a sudden awareness of what he must be imagining. She had just seen her ex-fiancé, she had reacted all too emotionally—and completely out of character when she'd asked to go back to Jonathan's home with him!— and Jonathan had to be thinking she had behaved in this way because she had just seen Richard. But that was only half the truth, it was all so much deeper than that.

'Why didn't you marry him?' Jonathan pressed, the question seemed to be forced out of him.

Whereas, in contrast, Gaye felt relaxed, somehow more relaxed than she had for a long time. 'Basically because I've always believed marriage is something to be shared between two people only,' she replied.

'Well, of course it— Craven had someone else in his

60

life at the same time he was engaged to you!' Jonathan realised angrily.

'Several someones, as it turned out,' she said dryly. 'As the lovingly trusting fiancée, I was the last to find out! As seems to be usual in these cases.' She grimaced ruefully.

Jonathan looked furious. 'I trust someone punched him on the nose for you?'

Gaye laughed softly, shaking her head, relieved to be able to laugh about it at last. 'No—but I believe the diamond in our engagement ring did leave an interesting cut on his cheek for several weeks after I threw it at him!'

Jonathan looked astounded at the image she'd created for him with her words. Causing Gaye to chuckle again. She really did feel lighter in her heart. She had seen Richard again, and although it had been hard to do she had faced him down with her silent refusal even to acknowledge she knew him, and she had done it all with the marvellously handsome Jonathan Hunter at her side. That was what had made the difference, she inwardly acknowledged.

Richard's duplicity, at a time when she had badly needed his support and strength, had been more than she could bear. But now, two years later, with Jonathan at her side, she had been able to face Richard without any hesitation or embarrassment on her part. The fact that Richard had felt no awkwardness in approaching her just confirmed what she had learnt only too forcibly two years ago: Richard Craven was a man without principles or honour. A self-orientated—

'Good for you.' Jonathan spoke warmly. 'But it isn't

too late to administer the punch on the nose too. Just say the word,' he offered.

'He isn't important enough to merit the attention,' Gaye responded, meaning every word. Richard was no longer important. For two years their broken engagement had been yet another open wound for her to deal with, but after seeing him again she realised he meant nothing to her. 'But thank you for the offer, anyway.' She smiled across at Jonathan again, feeling somehow as if she was looking at him for the first time.

What an absolutely gorgeous man he was! Not just good-looking—Richard was good-looking!—Jonathan was breathtaking! Tall, blond, with those amazing golden-coloured eyes, he had to be the most handsome man Gaye had ever seen.

Somehow he had become the key to releasing all her pain. She had held the tears in for so long, but almost from the first time she'd met Jonathan she had felt those tears threatening to fall, finally culminating in that outburst minutes ago. Why Jonathan Hunter, a man so out of her reach, in so many ways…?

'Is he the one?' Jonathan asked gruffly at her side. 'The one who told you you're an infuriating woman?' he explained as she frowned her puzzlement.

Her frown disappeared, her smile poignant now. 'No,' she assured him huskily. 'That was my father.'

Jonathan stared at her. 'Your father…?'

She gave a half-smile. 'My father,' she nodded. 'Nursing, with all its hardships, was the last thing he had in mind for me as a career.'

'But I'm sure he's proud of you now,' Jonathan said assuredly.

She drew in a ragged breath. 'He was,' she told him

chokily. 'He died two years ago,' she supplied at his questioning look.

'I'm sorry. I didn't— Oh, hell,' Jonathan muttered uncomfortably. 'But he must have been very young?'

'Probably not as young as you might imagine,' she said, her voice thick with emotion. 'As he was fond of telling me, I was rather an afterthought to a marriage that had already been successful for almost twenty years!'

Jonathan whistled through his teeth. 'That was some afterthought!'

'Yes,' Gaye agreed. 'I had the most marvellous childhood, was thoroughly spoilt by over-indulgent parents.' She blinked back the tears at the thought of those happy memories. 'My parents were wonderful.'

'Were? Is your mother dead, too?' Jonathan rejoined with feeling.

She gave a pained look. No, her mother wasn't dead, but the true essence of her, Terence's wife, Gaye's mother—that person was no longer there...

'No,' Gaye assured him distantly, realising that perhaps, in those initial feelings of relief at having got through seeing Richard again, she had said too much. It had been so long since she had spoken to anyone about these things... 'I— Do you have parents?' She changed the subject, realising by the way he was suddenly the one filled with tension that she had touched upon a difficult subject for him now.

Why did things have to be so complicated? Maybe that was why, although she now deeply regretted that lapse, she had asked to go home with him a short time ago, not to talk, but simply to feel. It seemed that conversation very often only confused things...

When she was a child her world had seemed so full
of sunshine, her parents at the centre of her golden uni-
verse. Oh, there had been the usual ups and downs of
puberty, the tears as well as the laughter, persuading her
father to accept the career she had chosen for herself: he
had wanted her to do something else completely. But he
had been so proud of her on the day she qualified,
thrilled with her subsequent specialisation of midwifery,
teasing her endlessly about her love of babies, sure that
it wouldn't be too long before she provided him with
grandchildren. But, like most fathers, he had considered
her choice of future husband not good enough for her—
and in Richard he had, if posthumously, been proven
correct! He never had become a grandfather...!

'Yes.' Jonathan suddenly answered the question Gaye
had almost forgotten she had asked—so long was his
answer in coming. 'They're divorced. My father lives in
Australia. I have no idea where my mother is,' he added
coldly.

The way he said it implied so much more than the
words themselves; there was a wealth of pain and bitterness behind them.

Gaye looked at him, gently searching, briefly seeing
the hurt in his eyes before it was quickly masked and
Jonathan forced himself to relax. That lazy charm hid a
much more complex man than he cared to admit, Gaye
realised...

'Jonathan—' She broke off from what she had been
about to say as the pub door opened and a noisy crowd
of people burst out onto the pavement—Richard
amongst them, Gaye noticed dispassionately.

She looked at him, unseen in the darkness of
Jonathan's car, saw the casual way Richard's arm was

draped about the shoulders of a tall redhead. In much the same way his arm used to be draped about Gaye's shoulders...

But she found she could look at Richard now with complete detachment. She had loved him once, to the point where she refused to listen to any of the words of caution given by her parents. But, looking at him now, she could only see a rather too good-looking man, the lines of dissipation already starting to show beside his eyes and mouth, could see the man who had used her and her family connections until they were no longer of any use to him.

She turned abruptly away from him, only to find Jonathan watching her with the same intensity with which she had looked at Richard, those golden eyes glowing in the semi-darkness of the car.

Gaye gave a small smile. 'Isn't it strange how sometimes you can look back and, in retrospect, give thanks for having been saved from a fate worse than death? Being Richard's wife,' she explained as Jonathan looked at her blankly. 'He married a year or so ago.'

She remembered how upsetting she had found it at the time to see his smiling face in the newspapers at the side of his new bride. 'That redhead certainly isn't his wife!' she added disgustedly. Marriage hadn't changed Richard in the least; she doubted anything ever would; to Richard there would always be a more beautiful, more advantageous woman just around the corner! She doubted he would ever stop looking for those women.

Jonathan chuckled softly at her side. 'You really *are* over him, aren't you?' he said with satisfaction.

She really was! But alarm bells had begun ringing in her head at Jonathan's obvious pleasure in the fact. Her life really was already complicated enough. Besides, Jonathan had mentioned that the newspapers followed his romantic life—and attracting publicity was the last thing she wanted to do. There had been enough of that!

She gave a dismissive smile. 'I'm over men. Period.'

He steadily met her gaze. 'If that remark is supposed to warn me off—'

'It isn't 'supposed' to do anything,' she interrupted sharply, knowing she had been right about those alarm bells. 'I'm stating a fact.'

'And I'm expected to believe you, after what happened between us earlier?' he scorned lightly. 'You're beautiful, Gaye. Responsive. Very warm and giving—when you want to be. I refuse to accept—'

'The Hunter arrogance won't work on me, Jonathan,' she cut in, breathing hard in her agitation.

This evening had turned out better than she had expected it would, that chance meeting with Richard included, but now she needed some time alone to sort things out in her mind, to put a new perspective on things. But it wouldn't include Jonathan!

She couldn't claim not to be attracted to him; that would be ridiculous after what had happened between them. But realising that part of her life, the part which had once included Richard, had somehow healed itself without her even being aware of it did not mean there was now room for someone like Jonathan. Richard had been a mistake; Jonathan would be a catastrophe!

'I'm afraid I have to go now—'

'You aren't afraid at all, Gaye.' Jonathan stopped her harshly. 'Who are you hurrying home to, Gaye?' he continued shrewdly. 'There has to be someone. I know

damn well you don't live in that big house all by yourself!'

She froze, staring at him with huge green eyes. 'What
on earth makes you think that?' she prompted breathlessly.

Jonathan shot her a chiding look. 'Give me credit for
some intelligence, Gaye; that house is too damned big
for just one person!'

For a moment she had wondered if he did, after all,
know more about her than he had let on; now she realised he was still guessing. But for how much longer…?

'You're absolutely right, Jonathan,' she answered him
calmly. 'I don't live alone. I live with my mother,' she
told him, taking care to keep her tone light. 'It really is
time I was getting back now,' she added with an osten-
tatious glance at her watch. 'My mother has been a little
nervous of being left alone in the house since my father
died.'

'But she can't be that old,' he insisted. 'And you said
it's been two years—'

'They were a very devoted couple,' Gaye defended.

'That doesn't mean that you, their only and afterthought child, have to devote your life to your mother—'
He broke off as Gaye began to laugh, staring at her,
bemused.

'I'm sorry.' She sobered slightly, though she still
smiled. 'But my mother would be horrified if she could
hear your description of her.' Gaye shook her head. 'My
mother may now be sixty-five, but she's still very fit and
beautiful. She certainly wouldn't welcome the thought
of being classed as elderly and in need of sympathy!'

'Then why—?'

'She wouldn't welcome it, Jonathan,' Gaye told him

firmly. 'But the truth of the matter is, she's very lonely, hates to be on her own.'

'Invite me to dinner,' he decided suddenly.

'What...?' Gaye looked startled.

'Invite me to dinner,' he repeated determinedly. 'That way your mother wouldn't be alone the next time we see each other—'

'Jonathan,' she interjected. 'There isn't going to be a next time. I certainly have no intention of inviting you home to meet my mother!' She inwardly shuddered at the thought.

'Why not? You've already met my family,' he reminded her confidently.

'Not your mother,' she countered, knowing she had scored a point as he stiffened. 'No, I'm sorry, Jonathan. I have no intention of either inviting you to dinner or to meet my mother!' Her mother would immediately start matchmaking, uncaring of the trouble Jonathan would bring to their lives, just by being who he was. 'Now I really do have to get home.' She reached for the door handle.

Jonathan reached over and stopped her, very close again now, his eyes dark as he looked at her. 'I'll drive you home,' he told her huskily. 'Don't refuse, Gaye,' he added softly as she was about to do just that. 'It's late, it's dark, and I'll feel better if I drive you home rather than you walk home alone.'

When he put it like that... 'Thank you,' she accepted.

Those golden eyes widened, Jonathan shaking his head, although he made no move to distance himself from her. 'I expected you to refuse,' he admitted.

Gaye met his gaze unblinkingly, although she was

barely breathing, very conscious of how close he still was. 'Did you want me to refuse?'

'Hell, no.' He straightened, chuckling softly as he turned on the ignition. 'I just thought— Maybe with you I shouldn't think too much; you're constantly surprising me!'

Not least of those surprises, she suspected, was her broken engagement to Richard! No doubt, when Jonathan took the time to think over this evening's conversations, as she was sure he would—Jonathan was by no means as laid-back and lazily charming as he liked to give the impression he was!—he would start to question how she could ever have met someone like Richard in the first place. On the face of it, the two of them must appear to have little in common!

But it was warm in the car, and comfortable, and for the moment Gaye allowed herself to relax during the short drive to her home. The home she shared with her mother...

Several lights were on inside the house when Jonathan turned the car into the driveway, not stopping at the end of it as he had the last time he drove her home, but driving right up to the front of the house, turning off the engine to get out of the car and come round to open her door for her.

'I'm sorry this evening didn't go off as smoothly for you as I might have wished,' he told her regretfully. 'But I want you to know that I've enjoyed myself.'

Funnily enough, so had she. She hadn't thought she would, had changed to come out this evening with deep feelings of trepidation, which was why she had made sure she was wearing clothes that she knew she looked good in and which gave her confidence; one thing she

had learnt was that she needed plenty of that around
Jonathan Hunter!

But even seeing Richard earlier hadn't put a dampener
on her enjoyment of Jonathan's company; in fact, seeing
Richard again, feeling completely free of him, had made
her appreciate Jonathan's attributes even more.

As for the time she had spent in his arms…!

'Thank you. So did I,' she returned directly. 'I—' She
broke off as the front door to the house opened, her heart
sinking as she saw her mother framed in the doorway.

'It is you, darling,' her mother greeted, her voice
warm and husky. 'I heard a car, and I—I'm so glad
Richard found you—' She broke off in confusion as she
focused on the man standing at Gaye's side and saw it
wasn't Richard at all. 'I'm most dreadfully sorry,' she
apologised to Jonathan. 'I thought you were someone
else.'

Gaye had been frozen to the spot where she stood
since the moment her mother opened the door, glancing
reluctantly at Jonathan from beneath long lashes. It was
dark, her mother had the light from the hallway behind
her; he might just not recognise her— But as Jonathan
stared at her mother with wide, disbelieving eyes Gaye
knew that her frantic hopes were all in vain—Jonathan
knew exactly who her mother was!

Why—oh, why—had her mother come to the door in
this way?

And exactly what did she mean about Richard finding
her? Had Richard been here earlier this evening, his arrival at The Swan not a chance meeting at all?

Gaye had an uneasy feeling in the pit of her stomach
at the thought of Richard being anywhere near her
mother. Why had he been here? What did he want?

More important at the moment, what was she going to say to Jonathan? Because, although he had been on the point of leaving, he now didn't look as if he intended going anywhere in the immediate future.

She couldn't say she blamed him...!

CHAPTER SIX

JONATHAN stared at Gaye's mother. He couldn't help it. That extraordinary figure, despite being in her mid-sixties, as Gaye had said her mother now was. That voice! Gaye had it too, he now realised: huskily sensual. And her mother's laugh too. And that glorious honey-blond hair.

This was all too incredible!

'Would you like to come in for coffee?' the beautiful vision in the doorway offered graciously. 'It's the least I can do after mistaking you for someone else,' she amended with an apologetic smile which lit up those amazing dark blue eyes.

Jonathan could feel Gaye at his side willing him to refuse. But there was no way he was going to be able to do what she wanted him to do. She was asking the impossible, and she must know that!

'You go ahead and make the coffee, Mummy.' Gaye quietly answered her mother for both of them. 'I'll be along with Jonathan in a moment.'

Another smile that dazzled, and Gaye's mother disappeared into the depths of the house. Presumably to make coffee.

Silence followed her departure; Jonathan simply couldn't speak, and Gaye obviously knew the reason he was dumbstruck. How could she not know?

Marilyn Palmer, the world-renowned actress, was Gaye's mother!

Jonathan had absolutely adored Marilyn Palmer when he was a teenager. Despite the fact that she had already been in her forties then, she had still dominated the stage and screen with her beauty and warmth, and it was the latter that had drawn Jonathan to her; he had always wondered, as he stared mesmerised up at the cinema screen, or at the television, why his own mother didn't possess any of the charisma the beautiful actress obviously did, why his own mother didn't laugh and look as happy.

But if Marilyn Palmer was Gaye's mother, then that obviously made— Royal…! Gaye had reacted so defensively earlier this evening when he had commented how unusual her name was; he hadn't meant the Royal part, but Gaye had taken it that he had…

'Terence Royal,' Gaye put in quietly as she seemed to read at least part of his jumbled thoughts. 'Yes, he was my father.' Her voice broke emotionally as she used the past tense to describe that tall, silver-haired man who had possessed such an air of distinction.

Terence Royal and Marilyn Palmer…

Two of the icons of film and theatre. The Golden Couple of acting. The couple had been married to each other for over forty years before Terence Royal was tragically killed in a car accident—

Jonathan looked sharply at Gaye, and he suddenly knew the reason she was so ethereal, so delicately lovely, the reason for the deep sadness in the deep green depths of her wonderful eyes. Her family, that 'most marvellous childhood', those 'over-indulgent' parents; it had all been shattered two years ago when her father died.

Plus, until two years ago, she had also been engaged to marry Richard Craven...

Gaye gave a wry smile as she watched the play of emotions flickering across Jonathan's face. 'You're running way ahead of me,' she said ruefully. 'My engagement ended on the night my father was killed because when I went to Richard's apartment to tell him the dreadful news I found him in bed with his current leading lady!'

She spoke tonelessly, but it didn't take too much sensitivity to realise the agony she must have gone through that night, to have lost her adored father, and then to find out her fiancé had betrayed her. Jonathan didn't just want to punch Richard Craven on the nose any more, he wanted to—

'My mother mentioned Richard when we arrived back,' Gaye continued distractedly. 'You don't think—'

'Let's go and ask her,' Jonathan decided grimly, taking a firm grip of Gaye's arm as he moved determinedly into the house.

Gaye resisted, looking up at him with cloudy green eyes. 'The— My— The accident changed my mother,' she finally told him slowly, her expression troubled.

He studied her searchingly, but as usual he learnt nothing from her expression. 'In what way?'

She trembled slightly in his grasp. 'In every way that matters!' she told him forcefully. 'Losing my father was a great shock to her. She—I— It's difficult to explain.'

'Then don't even try,' Jonathan soothed, squeezing her arm reassuringly. 'Believe it or not, I'm a relatively intelligent man—when I'm not around you. But you come on the scene—and I start acting like all kinds of an idiot!' he confessed. 'But I promise you I won't do or say anything that will upset your mother,' he added seriously. 'Now let's go inside and have that coffee before your mother wonders where we've got to!'

He could still sense Gaye's reluctance, but in the circumstances she really had no choice but to comply, leading the way into the elegantly beautiful home, with its restful green and gold decor, and wonderfully ornate antique furniture.

Jonathan would have expected nothing less from the gloriously beautiful Marilyn Palmer, or indeed from Gaye either; both women possessed a natural style and elegance of their own. As Gaye led him into what was obviously the family sitting room he found himself bombarded with dozens of photographs of Marilyn Palmer and Terence Royal, from their first years together, through their early marriage, and then into Gaye's childhood. A smiling, laughing, totally worshipped Gaye, deep pride and love in both her parents' eyes as they proudly looked on, both, it seemed, happy to allow their own precious little star to steal the limelight away from them, two people who were adored the world over.

Gaye was right—her parents had been a very devoted couple, and it was obvious that she had been included in that devotion from the day she was born. But two years ago her father had died.

Jonathan had never been lucky enough to meet Terence Royal, but his presence on stage and screen could be tangibly felt. Jonathan had a feeling it had been the same here in his home and family. These two women had lost so much more than a husband and father...

Gaye seemed to have survived the loss, in her own way, but Marilyn— He was beginning to guess at the trauma her husband's death might have caused her.

'It will be all right, Gaye,' Jonathan reassured her as she stood stiffly just inside the room, looking as if 'all right' was the last thing it was going to be! 'I'll drink my coffee and then go. We can sit and talk about all of this tomorrow evening—over dinner,' he added softly.

Gaye looked across at him with raised brows, her lips pursing wryly. 'Opportunist,' she muttered without rancour.

'That's me,' Jonathan accepted with an easy smile.

'In this case I can't exactly say I blame you,' Gaye admitted. 'If I were in your shoes…'

'But you aren't, so don't worry about it,' he assured her as he could hear her mother coming down the hallway. 'Now let's all just have a pleasant cup of coffee together. I promise I won't outstay my welcome,' he said as Gaye still looked far from happy.

As Marilyn Palmer entered the room with the coffee-tray, he knew that promise was going to be hard to keep; the older woman was absolutely mesmerising, her movements fluid and confident, the smile she gave him radiant as he moved to take the laden tray from her.

'This is Jonathan Hunter, Mummy,' Gaye introduced lightly. 'A friend of mine,' she added firmly.

'It's lovely to meet you,' Marilyn told him in genuine welcome, allowing her hand to be briefly taken once Jonathan had put the tray down on the low table in front of the sofa. 'We have so few visitors nowadays,' she reflected wistfully.

He found that surprising, he had to admit, knew that as a couple Marilyn Palmer and Terence Royal had been courted by royalty as well as fellow actors. But they weren't a couple any more, and some people, he knew, found it difficult to be around the bereaved. But even so—

'You said something about Richard having called round earlier, Mummy,' Gaye prompted smoothly as she poured the coffee for the three of them.

'Oh, yes.' Marilyn sat down in one of the armchairs.

Although merely to say she sat was to understate the movement totally, Jonathan realised with fascination. Marilyn didn't just sit, she glided, each movement graceful, the fitted dress she wore a perfect match in blue for the darkness of her eyes.

'Such a surprise, darling.' Marilyn continued to talk to Gaye, her face as youthful and unlined as it had been twenty years ago. 'He was so sorry to have missed you.'

Gaye handed her mother a cup of black coffee. 'What did he want?' she enquired casually.

Although Jonathan could see her nervousness as she sat on the edge of her chair, her shoulders hunched stiffly. He suddenly had an overwhelming urge to go and stand behind her chair and massage the tension out of those shoulders and that lovely delicate neck.

Wonderful! So much for his promise to drink his coffee and go; he didn't want to go at all; he wanted Gaye to sit next to him on the sofa where he now sat alone, for the two of them to talk softly together, and then for them to go upstairs and—

He sat forward himself as the stirrings of his body threatened to betray him. Excellent! If his mind continued along this path much longer then he wasn't going to be able to stand up and leave when the time came!

'Thank you.' He took his own cup of coffee, avoiding Gaye's gaze as she gave it to him. For the moment it would be better if he didn't even look at her!

'He wanted to see you, of course, darling,' her mother answered her happily. 'I realise the two of you have had a little falling-out, but Richard obviously regrets it, and he did look so sorry to have missed you. I didn't think you would mind if I told him where you were. Of course, I had no idea you were with Jonathan.' She gave him an apologetic smile. 'I hope I didn't cause anyone any embarrassment!'

'Certainly not on my account,' Jonathan assured her smoothly, still caught up in the 'little falling-out' remark; finding your fiancé in bed with another woman was a major falling-out in his book!

'Or mine,' Gaye added softly. 'Richard didn't say anything else?' Even now, Jonathan noticed, she didn't sit back in her seat, still poised on the edge of it, as if ready for flight.

'Oh, he did mention a script I might like to have a look at,' her mother threw in breezily. 'Some play or other that he's thinking of directing.'

The hand that held Gaye's coffee-cup shook slightly now. 'That's new,' she said warily. 'He always said directing was a thankless job.'

'Oh, it is, darling,' her mother agreed with feeling. 'The one and only time your father directed he said he would never do it again. For which I am very grateful,' she added with a breathless laugh. 'He was impossible to live with for weeks!'

'What did you say to Richard about doing the play, Mummy?' Gaye pressed tensely.

'You know I never do any role without your father's approval, Gaye, darling,' her mother chided with light rebuke. 'I told him to contact your father, of course.'

It was as well Jonathan wasn't in the process of sipping his coffee at that moment, or he would have choked on it. Talk to Gaye's father? To Terence Royal? But—

He looked across at Marilyn Palmer searchingly, now seeing beyond the warm beauty, the glittering charm, noticing for the first time the slight vacancy in those deep blue eyes, a total lack of anything but smiling good humour. No matter how Jonathan might have longed for just such a mother himself when he was growing up, he also knew it wasn't realistic for someone to be always smiling and happy...

This was what Gaye had meant about her mother being different since Terence Royal died; to Marilyn her husband wasn't dead!

Gaye nodded in answer to her mother's last comment, studiously avoiding looking at Jonathan. 'I'll speak to Richard myself,' she said quickly.

Like hell she would! Her mother might have chosen to shut out all the pain and sudden emptiness of two years ago by pretending it had never happened, but Gaye and Jonathan were well aware of Richard Craven's betrayal at that time, and his subsequent marriage to someone else. A wife he was now cheating on with someone else. Jonathan had no intention of Gaye ever going near that man again if he could avoid it. And he had every intention of doing so!

How on earth had Gaye coped with all of this alone for the last two years?

God, no wonder she had asked to go home with him an hour ago; he would want to escape for a few hours too if he had to carry this burden by himself. Except Gaye wasn't on her own any more... She might not want it, or like it, but he was in her life now. He didn't intend going anywhere else in the immediate future.

'*We'll* speak to Richard for you together,' he put in firmly, levelly meeting Gaye's accusing gaze as she turned sharply to him.

Marilyn looked momentarily confused as she looked at him, and then she seemed to dismiss the puzzle of Jonathan being with Gaye—as she must have dismissed a lot of things going on around her during the last two years if they appeared to disturb the fragile balance of a mind practising the most severe denial. Not least of those things being the fact that her husband, a man she had obviously adored, was in fact dead! Jonathan couldn't even begin to fathom how she managed to do that; it would take an expert in such matters to understand it. An expert Jonathan intended speaking to at the earliest opportunity!

'It will be dealt with,' Gaye reassured her mother enigmatically.

At least, to Marilyn it might have been enigmatic, but it told Jonathan all too clearly that Gaye did not intend him to be involved in this any further, certainly not to the point of accompanying her when she talked to Richard Craven.

'Wonderful,' Marilyn agreed, rising gracefully to her feet. 'I'll leave you two young people now to finish your coffee.' She put her empty cup down on the tray. 'It was lovely to meet you, Jonathan,' she told him pleasantly. 'Please do come again.'

He nodded. 'Oh, I intend to.' It was a promise, not an empty statement.

'I'll look forward to it,' Marilyn told him with husky pleasure. 'Do invite Jonathan to dinner one evening, darling,' she said to Gaye as she bent to kiss her goodnight. 'It would be wonderful to start entertaining again,' she added wistfully before leaving the room, taking her life and vitality with her, leaving behind only her heady perfume.

And Gaye who, Jonathan noted with a frown, looked on the edge of exhaustion.

'Drink your coffee,' he advised abruptly, standing up to move closer to her chair.

She looked up at him with eyes too large and luminous a green in that ethereally beautiful face. 'I—' She stopped, drawing in a deep breath. 'It— She—' Gaye shook her head, unable to go on.

Jonathan leant down, reaching out and pulling Gaye effortlessly up beside him, taking her gently into his arms. 'It *will* be all right, Gaye,' he comforted her.

She looked up at him with tear-wet eyes.

'It will, Gaye.' His arms tightened about her at her look of disbelief. 'I'll make sure it is.'

And he would. He didn't know how yet, but he would find a way. He had to!

As his hands cradled each side of Gaye's face, as his mouth moved slowly down to claim hers, he had no idea why he was so determined to help this woman.

As their lips fused heatedly together, he found he didn't care about the reasons why…!

CHAPTER SEVEN

A SOB caught in Gaye's throat as her arms moved up over Jonathan's shoulders, her fingers becoming entangled in the silky blondness of the hair at his nape. She wanted to lose herself again, forget for a few moments; yes, she definitely felt freer than she had in ages. Jonathan was going to help her. She didn't know how, couldn't even begin to guess why, but she suddenly felt that everything was going to be all right.

For now, in Jonathan's arms, everything was all right.

Jonathan was holding her, kissing her, and that felt so right.

More right than it ever had with Richard?

She came down to earth with a thump at the thought of her ex-fiancé. Richard... He had been here earlier this evening, and his presence in the bar later hadn't been an accident, and that show of surprise at seeing her had all been an act. Because he had been here first and spoken to her mother.

Gaye pulled back from Jonathan, apology in her expression as she looked up at him. But there was also apprehension. They had a housekeeper who came in daily when Gaye was at work, and who kept unwanted visitors away from her mother. In the evenings Gaye was here to shield her mother as best she could. But the system had broken down this evening with Gaye's absence from the house...

'You're thinking about Craven again,' Jonathan

rasped harshly, his hands falling back to his sides, his expression grim.

'He will have realised from talking to my mother that she—well, that she still isn't well.'

'And you think he may use that information?' Jonathan frowned darkly.

The Richard she had once believed herself in love with had been handsome, charming, full of fun and laughter, but the Richard she had later come to know was egotistical, selfish, ambitious, and completely ruthless.

The fact that Gaye had found out he was involved with other women during their engagement hadn't meant a great deal to him. With her father dead, and her mother ill, they were no longer of any use to him in furthering his career, and in consequence neither was Gaye.

The breaking of their engagement had meant nothing to him; he'd moved on swiftly, his next relationship with the daughter of a director he had long wanted to work with. The release of the film that followed had put him well on the road to stardom. But the daughter of the director had duly been replaced by yet another woman he could use to step on on his way up the ladder of success. Richard had put a whole new meaning on the phrase 'casting couch'!

However, he had talked to her mother earlier about directing. His obvious coup would be to bring Marilyn Palmer back to the theatre!

Gaye would have welcomed her mother's return to acting, a world her mother had always adored, and which adored her, but not under these circumstances. She wouldn't allow her mother to be used by Richard, of all people!

'He'll use anything if he can,' Gaye answered
Jonathan cynically. 'But I don't aim to let him!'

'*We* don't aim to let him,' Jonathan corrected her
firmly. 'I meant what I said to your mother earlier,
Gaye,' he went on determinedly. 'You aren't in this on
your own any more.'

She swallowed hard. It had been so long since anyone
had wanted to help her. Her own fault; she realised that.
Her parents' acting friends had been very attentive during those first few months after the accident that killed
her father, the letters, cards and flowers all acknowledged by her, the telephone calls and personal calls
much harder to deal with. Especially as it had become
obvious, as the weeks and months passed, that her
mother, although now fully physically recovered from
her own injuries in the accident, was somehow trapped
in a time-warp—where husband, Terence Royal, was
still alive!

The personal visits had stopped, the telephone calls
too when it became obvious Marilyn would not be returning to work in the near future, if ever. The two
women had become isolated, with Gaye protecting her
mother in every way that she could, and that included
spending most of her time with her. Money was no problem, her parents having amassed a fortune over their
years of acting. But the isolation had become a problem,
until the doctors had recommended that Gaye go back
to work and employ a housekeeper to be at the house
with her mother during the day. It wasn't an ideal arrangement, with Gaye still constantly worrying about her
mother when she was out, but it had muddled along quite
comfortably for the last six months.

Until tonight. The first evening Gaye had spent away

from her mother, Richard Craven had burst back into their lives. He had backed off earlier at the pub, probably because of Jonathan's presence, but, knowing him of old, Gaye realised Richard would be back! He obviously had some sort of plan in mind, and he wouldn't give up on it easily.

'Why are you so interested, Jonathan?' she said brightly.

His mouth tightened. 'You're being insulting, Gaye,' he rasped.

'I don't mean to be,' she replied. 'More coffee?' she offered, leaning forward to lift the pot.

'Thanks.' He pushed his cup across to her. 'You may not mean to be insulting, Gaye—' although his tone said he doubted that '—but you most certainly are. I'm in this with you now.'

She looked at him with candid green eyes. 'Why?'

'What do you mean—why?' he exploded, his coffee forgotten on the table as he paced the room. 'You can't expect me to just walk away from this, not now I know—now I realise—'

'That my mother is Marilyn Palmer,' Gaye finished for him, shaking her head in gentle rebuke.

'Who your mother is has nothing to do with it,' Jonathan bit out harshly, eyes glittering deeply gold.

'Of course it does,' Gaye chided, sitting down again.

It had been the same all her life, first at school, then during her nurse's training, at the hospital where she went to work once she had qualified; people were always amazed, and then intrigued, by the fact that her mother was Marilyn Palmer and her father was Terence Royal. Most had wondered why, with two such notable and obviously wealthy parents, Gaye had bothered to work at all, let alone at something that could be so arduous. None could believe that, as the daughter of two such talented actors, Gaye had no dramatic ability herself. But it was true. As numerous teachers had learnt to their cost during her years at school!

'You won't be the first young man to be in love with my mother,' Gaye assured Jonathan dryly; that too had been happening most of her adult life. But, as she also thought her mother was the most beautiful, as well as lovely-natured, woman, Gaye could quite understand why!

'I am not in love with—' Jonathan broke off his angry outburst, glaring at her fiercely. 'Yes, I've admired her since I was in my teens, possibly lusted after her a little then too, but that sort of hero-worship stopped being part of my life when I was sixteen, and my father went bankrupt and my mother walked out on all of us! There was no money then for the theatre or cinema, let alone the time or inclination. Who your mother is has nothing at all to do with my involvement now,' he insisted.

Gaye barely heard the last statement, still caught up in the previous ones. He had mentioned before that he didn't know where his mother was, and she had had no idea she had left under such awful circumstances. She had just assumed that the Hunters had always had money, that Jonathan was basically a rich playboy. She was wrong...

'I appreciate your concern, Jonathan— Yes, I do,' she said sincerely at his sceptical snort of disbelief. 'But I really don't see what you can do that hasn't already been done. We've seen doctors, specialists; money has been no object—but my mother simply refuses to accept that my father is dead.' Her voice broke over those last four words.

'What about you?' Jonathan prompted softly.

She looked at him sharply. 'Oh, I know he's dead,' she said flatly.

She had always adored her father, neither of her parents excluding their only child with the love they had for each other. She had been almost as devastated as her mother when her father was killed. Almost...

'My father died instantly in the accident, and my mother was trapped in the car beside him for hours after it happened, her legs trapped,' she told Jonathan dully. 'Is it any wonder that her brain refuses to acknowledge those hours?' She looked across at him with haunted eyes.

'No,' he acknowledged gruffly, moving down on his haunches beside her chair. 'But, as you've pointed out to me already this evening, your mother is only in her mid-sixties—it's impossible to contemplate her continuing to live like this, or you either, for another twenty years! Let me help you, Gaye.' He reached out and tightly grasped her hands in his. 'Let me help her,' he added with feeling.

She swallowed hard. It had been so long since anyone had wanted to help...!

'You're a busy man, Jonathan—'

'Not so busy I don't have time to help a friend,' he cut in.

A friend... Somehow Gaye felt a sense of disappointment at the thought of only ever being this man's 'friend'. The fact that he'd been at her side this evening when she'd met Richard had given her a freedom she might otherwise not have felt. And it wasn't, she realised now, just because she had been with a handsome, obviously worldly man. Jonathan himself gave her a confidence that had been lacking from her life the last couple of years, a confidence in the future. If anyone could help her mother, then she had a feeling Jonathan was that person. And, in doing so, he would help her too...

But what about after that? Would Jonathan just leave their lives then, or would he continue to be their 'friend'?

Because she was fast coming to the conclusion she didn't want him to leave her life.

To feel that way was a mistake, she was sure. She knew little about the Hunter men, but what was obvious was that they were all in their thirties, and of the three of them only Jarrett had married, only two years ago. Maybe she had been given an insight into the reason for that a few minutes ago; the brothers had been deserted by their mother at a very impressionable age, so it was no wonder that none of them had too much trust in women! Although, a brave little voice inside her head said, Jarrett had overcome that lack of trust when he fell in love with Abbie, so why should it be impossible for Jonathan to do the same? If he ever fell in love...

Trust. It was something she didn't have too much of either, not after Richard's multiple unfaithfulnesses.

'In that case—' she squeezed his hand '—I accept your offer of help.'

He blinked, looking at her in complete amazement. 'This is getting to be quite a habit of yours. Every time I think I have a battle on my hands, you give in without further argument!' he explained dazedly.

She laughed at his bemused expression. 'My father

told me long ago to fight the fights that need fighting, and be gracious in defeat over the ones that don't.'

Jonathan gave a regretful sigh. 'I would have liked him,' he said.

Her father would have approved of Jonathan too; of that she was sure. He would have liked Jonathan's strength, his sense of fun, and that certain old-fashioned chivalry, which her father had also possessed, but which Jonathan probably wasn't even aware of in himself.

Yes, her father would have liked Jonathan. As he had never approved of Richard.

It had been one of the few things she and her father had ever disagreed on, her father suspicious from the first concerning the younger man's apparent devotion. In the end her father had proved much wiser than her...

'My mother suggested inviting you to dinner.' She deliberately shrugged off her melancholy thoughts; they achieved nothing, either. 'Which evening would be convenient for you?'

He seemed to give the matter some thought, and Gaye realised that perhaps she was being too presumptuous. Jonathan was, after all, a very attractive man, would be socially much in demand, and although he denied any serious relationship in his life she very much doubted that he spent all of his evenings alone. His nights, either...

'You don't have to decide now,' she amended quickly. 'Your sister-in-law will be in the clinic for another day or so; you can easily let me know about dinner when you come in to visit her. I don't suppose for one minute—'

'Gaye—you're babbling,' Jonathan interrupted with calm amusement. 'Dinner is a good idea. And any evening will be convenient,' he informed her dryly, eyes twinkling mischievously, as if all too aware of what she had been thinking concerning his private life. 'I was merely thinking further along the line—running before I can walk, my big brother would call it.' He grimaced. 'I have an idea, but I need to speak to some people first before I attempt to put it into action.' He straightened. 'In the meantime, dinner tomorrow evening will be fine.'

What idea? What people did he need to talk to before telling her about it?

Gaye had a fleeting flashback of memory, to the moment Jarrett Hunter had marched arrogantly into the operating Theatre to be with his wife—and realised that Jonathan possessed that same arrogance, albeit usually hidden behind that lazy charm.

She had the sudden feeling of standing in the path of an express train—and hoping it wouldn't run her down!

Except that she was the one who had released the brake and started that train on its way…!

She hadn't even left the house for work the next morning when the telephone rang. Jonathan wasn't wasting any time!

She had taken a breakfast tray up to her mother earlier, and Mrs Charles had arrived fifteen minutes ago, leaving Gaye ten minutes to get to the bus stop. This was not the time for Jonathan to be calling her!

She almost dropped the receiver when Richard responded to her brief hello!

'Gaye!' he greeted jovially. 'This time I know it has to be you.'

She recovered quickly from her surprise; why should she be at all taken aback? Richard could be as tenacious as Jonathan when there was something he wanted—and he wanted her mother to star in the play he intended directing!

'You knew it was me last night, Richard,' she returned scornfully. 'And isn't this rather early in the morning for you to be out of bed?' she added caustically, remembering all too well how he didn't consider the day started until after midday!

'I'm filming at the moment,' he returned lightly. 'I must say, the theatre has its compensations!'

'What do you want, Richard?' Gaye prompted coldly. 'You—' She broke off as the doorbell rang down the hallway, shooting Mrs Charles a grateful smile as the housekeeper went to answer the door. It was seldom nowadays that either the telephone or the doorbell rang, let alone at the same time! 'You should not have come here last night, Richard,' she continued harshly. 'You have no right—'

'Your mother seemed pleased to see me,' he returned unabashedly.

Gaye's mouth tightened. 'Stay away from my mother, Richard—' She broke off again as the receiver was firmly and deliberately plucked out of her hand, eyes wide as she found herself looking up into Jonathan's grimly set features. He must have been the one ringing the doorbell, she realised dazedly.

'And stay away from Gaye, too,' Jonathan barked into the receiver. 'It certainly is,' he responded hardly to Richard's query. 'Where do I fit into the picture?' He mused softly over the other man's question, but the hardness of those glittering golden eyes told of his anger. 'I *am* the picture, Craven,' he stated harshly. 'Gaye and Marilyn are my concern now, and I advise you to stay away from both of them.' The threat in his tone was more than obvious before he slammed the receiver firmly back down in its cradle.

Gaye felt as stunned as the housekeeper looked as she hurried past the two of them on her way back to the kitchen.

Obviously Jonathan had heard Gaye on the telephone when the door was opened to him, and it hadn't taken him long to realise exactly who she was talking to, but nevertheless his cavalier attitude in taking over the call, in issuing veiled but definite threats, and implying a relationship between the two of them, was quite extraordinary.

As he stood so tensely beside her, anger was exuding from every pore of his body, but as Gaye considered she was the one with the right to be angry she really wasn't interested in his feelings. Besides, what on earth was he doing here at this time of the morning, in the first place?

'I'm here to save you the bother of buses and trains,' he rasped, the first indication Gaye had that she had spoken her thoughts out loud. 'Although perhaps I'm too late and lover-boy was going to drive you to work before I informed him otherwise?' He looked at her challengingly.

Gaye stared at him wordlessly. He was behaving ridiculously. He had to know, from the part of her conversation with Richard that he must have overheard when he arrived, that she hadn't been about to accept a lift from Richard—even if one had been forthcoming, which it hadn't!—or anything else!

What on earth was the matter with him?

CHAPTER EIGHT

HE WAS behaving ridiculously. Jonathan knew it, but there was nothing, it seemed, that he could do about it.

He had been awake half the night, first making telephone calls, and then discussing the problem with Jarrett—who was sworn to secrecy concerning Gaye's mother. Although, as Jonathan knew only too well, his older brother had always kept his own counsel.

But lack of sleep wasn't the whole reason for his outburst just now; he had been filled with fury when he'd arrived a few minutes ago to realise Gaye was actually talking on the telephone to Richard Craven, her ex-fiancé.

Jealousy was a totally alien emotion to Jonathan, an emotion he had never felt, let alone admitted to, but the first thought that had flashed through his mind earlier was, had Gaye initiated the telephone call or had Craven? If it was the latter, then the man had a colossal cheek, but if it had been the former—!

His anger rekindled anew at the thought of Gaye deliberately telephoning Richard. 'Why the hell don't you have a car and drive yourself to work?' he rasped accusingly. 'It would save all this damned inconvenience!'

Her head went back proudly, and Jonathan had to stop himself from lingering over the fact that Gaye looked absolutely beautiful this morning. It was a lovely day outside, and Gaye was dressed appropriately, the knee-length of her dark green sundress revealing part of the long expanse of her suntanned legs. She wore little make-up, her skin naturally creamy and soft, her hair once again loose about her shoulders and down her back, silkily gold. In fact, she looked too damned beautiful to travel on public transport, prey to the ogling of every man she came into contact with. If he had his way, he would lock her up and—

Now he was being ridiculous again! The days of keeping a woman hidden from other men, the wearing of chastity belts, were long gone. Besides, his name was Hunter, not Knight! Although he was starting to question uneasily who was the captive in this relationship—himself or Gaye...

'Never mind that for now.' He gave an impatient glance at his wristwatch. 'If you're ready to leave I suggest we do so.'

She looked as if she would have liked to refuse, but another glance at his grimly set features had her turning to pick up her bag and sling it over her shoulder before she preceded him to the door, obviously ready to leave.

He even liked that about her. Not only did she use her own initiative to decide when and when not to fight, but she also didn't fuss about her appearance, didn't even pause on her way down the hallway to glance in the mirror to check that she looked okay. Of course, he acknowledged with a glimmer of amusement as he followed her out to his car, that could be because she was just too angry at this moment!

'To answer your question—' she spoke quietly once they were in the car and Jonathan was driving in the direction of the clinic—the first time she had actually spoken since his arrival, Jonathan realised with surprise

'—I don't drive myself to and from work for the simple reason that I don't drive.'

Jonathan stared at her. What did she mean, she didn't drive? She didn't drive because she didn't want to—perhaps the scar she carried from the accident that had killed her father?—or she didn't drive because she couldn't? He couldn't believe it was the last, had never met anyone of—what must she be, twenty-six or seven?—who hadn't learnt to drive. She—

Gaye laughed at his obviously dumbfounded expression. That wonderful tinkling laugh that he found so entertaining.

'I think you had better turn your attention back to the road,' she advised teasingly. 'Otherwise you may not be driving for much longer, either!'

He instantly returned his attention to the road ahead, braking slowly as the car in front stopped at traffic lights. 'Why is it you don't drive?' he finally asked.

'I never learnt,' she responded. 'There was never any reason for me to do so. I've lived in London all my life, and it's always been easier, when necessary, to use public transport. And if there was ever a problem with that—' She broke off, turning to look out of the car window. 'Daddy drove,' she said flatly. 'And he never minded driving me if there was somewhere I had to be.'

He should have known. Should have guessed. He was behaving like the worst of idiots this morning. And now he had really hurt Gaye with his thoughtlessness. When that was the very last thing he wanted to do...

He reached across and lightly gripped her clasped hands. 'Well, I'm here to drive you now. If there's somewhere you need to be,' he added huskily. 'But I'll tell you something else, Gaye—the first thing we're going to do is get you some driving lessons!'

She turned big green eyes on him. 'Making sure you don't have to drive me for too long?' she mocked.

He was quite happy to be there for her, whenever she needed him, as her father had obviously been. But he just had a feeling, from what he had come to know of Gaye, that she would rather have her independence now than depend on other people. There just wouldn't have been the time in the last two years, since her father's death and her mother's emotional denial of that death, for Gaye to do anything for herself...

Jonathan smiled. 'Accuse me of that in three months when you have your licence and can drive yourself!'

'My father was always going to— But there was never the time—they were always so busy working, you see,' she concluded softly. 'Thank you,' she said chokily.

Jonathan didn't have to look at her to know that again, there were tears in her eyes. Or that those tears had been a luxury she simply couldn't afford for the past two years. As a lot of things emotional had been...

'I suggest you try and tell me that again after I've given you a lesson or two,' he told her dryly. 'I taught Jordan to drive years ago, and he tells me I'm a lousy teacher, have no patience, don't listen—'

'You intend teaching me yourself...?' Her surprise— and pleasure were evident in her voice.

Jonathan glanced at her, his eyes glinting wickedly. 'You have it on Jordan's authority that I'm not doing you any favours, Gaye,' he assured her humorously. 'But I can tell you you'll be ready to pass your test in three months' time,' he added with satisfaction. 'In fact, the

WELCOME TO THE CASINO!

**Try your luck at the Roulette Wheel ...
Play a hand of Twenty-One!**

How to play:

1. Play the Roulette and Twenty-One scratch-off games, as instructed on the opposite page, to see that you are eligible for FREE BOOKS and a FREE GIFT!

2. Send back the card and you'll receive TWO brand-new Harlequin Presents® novels. These books have a cover price of $3.75 each in the U.S. and $4.25 each in Canada, but they are yours to keep absolutely free.

3. There's no catch. You're under no obligation to buy anything. We charge nothing — ZERO — for your first shipment. And you don't have to make any minimum number of purchases — not even one!

4. The fact is, thousands of readers enjoy receiving books by mail from the Harlequin Reader Service® before they're available in stores. They like the convenience of home delivery, and they love our discount prices!

5. We hope that after receiving your free books you'll want to remain a subscriber. But the choice is yours — to continue or cancel, any time at all!

So why not take us up on our invitation, with no risk of any kind. You'll be glad you did!

*Play Twenty-One For This
Exquisite Free Gift!*

**THIS SURPRISE
MYSTERY GIFT
WILL BE YOURS
FREE WHEN YOU PLAY
TWENTY-ONE**

It's fun, and we're giving away *FREE GIFTS* to all players!

The Harlequin Reader Service® — Here's how it works:

Accepting your 2 free books and mystery gift places you under no obligation to buy anything. You may keep the books and gift and return the shipping statement marked "cancel." If you do not cancel, about a month later we'll send you 6 additional novels and bill you just $3.12 each in the U.S., or $3.49 each in Canada, plus 25¢ delivery per book and applicable taxes if any.* That's the complete price and — compared to the cover price of $3.75 in the U.S. and $4.25 in Canada — it's quite a bargain! You may cancel at any time, but if you choose to continue, every month we'll send you 6 more books, which you may either purchase at the discount price or return to us and cancel your subscription.

*Terms and prices subject to change without notice. Sales tax applicable in N.Y. Canadian residents will be charged applicable provincial taxes and GST.

If offer card is missing write to: Harlequin Reader Service, 3010 Walden Ave., P.O. Box 1867, Buffalo, NY 14240-9952

BUSINESS REPLY MAIL
FIRST-CLASS MAIL   PERMIT NO 717   BUFFALO NY

POSTAGE WILL BE PAID BY ADDRESSEE

HARLEQUIN READER SERVICE
3010 WALDEN AVE
PO BOX 1867
BUFFALO NY 14240-9952

NO POSTAGE
NECESSARY
IF MAILED
IN THE
UNITED STATES

first thing I'll do when I get into my office today is apply for your test date.'

Gaye shook her head. 'You're going way too fast for me.'

He had the feeling he had been doing that since the day he met her! But especially so this morning, since he had turned up so unexpectedly.

His jaw set as he recalled the fact that he had found her on the telephone to Craven when he'd arrived earlier. He still didn't know which one of them had instigated the call!

'It's my way,' he rasped harshly—more harshly than he meant to, cursing himself as he saw those peachy-cream cheeks go pale.

Damn—the last thing he wanted to do was upset her. The problem was, he seemed to succeed in doing exactly that most of the time!

'Dinner tonight.' He speedily changed the subject. 'I'll be bringing a friend with me.'

'No!' she protested instantly, turning in her seat to look at him. 'My mother isn't ready yet to—'

'We don't know what your mother is ready for yet, Gaye,' Jonathan said soothingly. 'After tonight we may be a little better informed.'

'Your friend is a psychiatrist,' Gaye realised heavily.

'Of a sort,' Jonathan answered guardedly.

Ben Travis was a psychiatrist, but his methods weren't always looked upon with approval by some of his peers. Jonathan had been at university with Ben's son, Sam, had met Ben several times on visits with Sam to his family home. It hadn't been easy to arrange for Ben to be present this evening; he was a busy man. But after talking with Jarrett for an hour the two brothers had decided Ben Travis was the person to help Marilyn, if anyone could. To Jonathan's surprise, and relief, it had turned out that Ben was available to join them for dinner tonight, and that he was very interested in meeting Gaye's mother.

'Trust me, Gaye.' Jonathan clasped her hands once again. 'At least let's try things my way for a while, hmm?'

She looked far from happy at the emotional pressure he was exerting, her mouth set stubbornly. 'If my mother appears in the least distressed by anything your friend says or does to her—'

'That won't happen, Gaye,' he assured her, impatient with the fact that they were almost at the clinic—and more than a little annoyed, he realised, that she wasn't more grateful for the help he was trying to give her.

What he had expected, he inwardly acknowledged, was that she would fling her arms around his neck in gratitude—a move that was totally impractical at the moment, besides being totally out of character for Gaye! Now he was being worse than ridiculous. Although it would have been nice...

Dream on, Hunter, he told himself.

'We'll arrive, eat dinner, chat—just chat, Gaye,' he continued hastily as she began to look upset again. 'And then the three of us will meet for lunch tomorrow and discuss the possibilities.' Depending on whether or not Ben considered anything could be done!

'Jonathan—'

'Gaye.' He had parked the car at the clinic now, turning towards her, his arm resting along the back of her seat. 'Fight the fights that need fighting,' he reminded her gently. 'And give in gracefully over the ones that don't!'

Her mouth quirked wryly. 'I did that earlier—over this lift to work,' she explained at his puzzled look. 'Your invitation was hardly polite, and I thought you extremely arrogant in taking over my telephone call—'

'But?' he protested—the reminder of her conversation with Craven wasn't helping his mood at all. So much for being the charming member of the Hunter family— it all went completely out the window when it came to this woman sitting at his side!

'But, as you pointed out at the time, it was a lift that saved me a lot of time and trouble,' she said frostily.

Jonathan looked at her wordlessly for several seconds, and then he burst out laughing. 'You know, Gaye, since meeting you I've developed a serious ego problem. It has a huge dent—if not hole—punched in it! I should have known you weren't going to let me off scotfree for being so arrogant!'

'Ah, but I did,' she reminded him.

'Only up to a point—*this* point,' he conceded. 'Why don't we reserve judgement on whether or not you need to fight me over my guest for dinner this evening, hmm?' He touched Gaye's cheek gently before turning to get out of the car. He walked round to open her door for her, locking the car behind them by remote control before taking a light grasp of her arm.

Gaye frowned up at him. 'Where are you going? I thought you were in a hurry?'

He grinned unabashedly. 'Now that I'm here I may as well pay Abbie and Conor a visit.'

Gaye's bemusement turned to irritation. 'I have a feeling either Abbie or I have been had—and please don't tell me which one.' She lifted a protesting hand as he would have spoken. 'Leave me with some illusions!'

'And you leave Abbie with some!' he returned laughingly. 'What time this evening, Gaye?' He sobered.

She drew in a deep breath, hesitating for several seconds, and then she slowly nodded—as if prepared, for the moment, to give him the benefit of the doubt! 'Seven-thirty or eight,' she decided. 'My mother is a stickler for formality, so if you and your friend could dress accordingly?'

Jonathan literally had to bite his bottom lip to stop a sharp retort; Gaye certainly wasn't making this easy for him. But then, he acknowledged with an inward grimace, it had been this very prickliness about her that had appealed to him in the first place. He couldn't have it both ways!

Not when he wanted Gaye any way he could get her...

His mouth twisted. 'I think we can manage that,' he said, coming to a halt outside Abbie's room. 'Is there anything you would like me to bring for this evening? For instance, the starter. Or some wines?'

Gaye declined softly. 'Thanks for the offer, but no. My mother has always loved to entertain, and as she has never liked caterers to come in I learnt to help her at a very young age. I think the two of us can manage to throw something together between us. Do you or your friend have any particular dislikes?'

As long as it wasn't him she threw he didn't care what they ate. 'None,' he assured her—unlike poor Jarrett, who had a definite aversion to shellfish, as it had an aversion to him!

'What about your friend?' she asked stiffly.

Still a touchy subject, he thought disappointedly. Well, it would have to be so; he was going to help these two lovely ladies even if it didn't win him any popularity contests!

'None that I'm aware of,' he said. 'If there are I'll let you know before tonight. Would you like me to come and pick you up after work?'

Gaye shook her head. 'You've already been helpful enough for one day, thank you,' she told him enigmatically. 'Besides, I have some shopping to do after work if we're to eat anything at all tonight.'

He frowned his consternation. 'I don't want to cause you any extra work with this dinner party.' He never entertained at home in his apartment, always took friends and family alike out to a restaurant to eat. He could throw together some simple meals for himself if he had to, but he very much doubted that was the sort of meal Gaye and her mother intended preparing for this evening. Damn, he simply hadn't thought of the extra work involved for her when he'd accepted the invitation! 'Maybe we could eat out— No,' he realised at a pointed glance from Gaye. 'Your mother wouldn't be able to cope with that just yet.' He gave a self-impatient frown. 'Damn, I haven't thought this thing through properly at all!' He had been so intent on spending time with Gaye, on helping Marilyn, and therefore Gaye too, that he hadn't given the logistics of dinner at their home too much thought.

'Leave the thinking to me, Jonathan.' Gaye put a placating hand on his arm. 'Just make sure you arrive on time this evening. And I promise you won't end up eating beans on toast!'

He barely repressed his expression of revulsion.

Baked beans he couldn't stand, after childhood meals put together by a mother who didn't really care what they ate, as long as they didn't whine about it. Jordan had been the one who liked baked beans, so the two boys had quickly learnt to swap something on Jordan's plate for the unwanted beans on Jonathan's. That way none of them had ended up in trouble for not eating the food their mother had 'taken the trouble to prepare'. Tipping the contents of a can into a saucepan, and letting them warm through, had never seemed particularly arduous to Jonathan, but by the time he was ten he had learnt to guard his tongue around his mother. Or pay the consequences!

Strange. He had thought more of his mother in the last few days than he could remember doing for years. Gaye's obvious closeness to her mother might have triggered it; the two women were obviously so close, as close as a mother and daughter could ever be, and yet he and his own mother—!

He hadn't even seen her for years, and he had no interest in doing so now, either. His mother had been married to her third husband the last time he heard of her ten years ago; as time passed, and her beauty had faded, so had the wealth of the men she had been able to cajole into marriage. He didn't doubt that one day he, Jarrett or Jordan would have a contrite mother on their doorstep hoping to live off the fortune they had amassed since she walked out on them over twenty years ago. His mother seemed even more repugnant than usual in the face of Gaye's relationship with her own mother...

'I was only joking, Jonathan.' Gaye seemed to have been watching the emotions flickering across his face, obviously concerned by his look of disgust.

It was an effort, but Jonathan forced himself to relax. Damn. He didn't want to think about his mother. In fact, he refused to do so any more.

'*You* leave the joking to me,' he returned lightly, 'and I'll leave the cooking to you! And try to look on this evening as a positive thing,' he advised more seriously. 'Hopefully, the first step towards your mother's recovery,' he encouraged.

'I'll try.' Gaye nodded slowly, although she still looked uncertain. 'I just don't want my mother upset in any way—'

'Ben Travis will not upset her, I can assure you of that,' Jonathan said with certainty. 'In fact, he's one of the most charming men I know. Your mother won't be able to help but like him— What is it?' he prompted as Gaye stared at him.

'I—I mistakenly thought your friend was a woman,' she finally explained awkwardly.

She had believed he was bringing a *woman* guest with him this evening! Could that possibly be the reason she had been so opposed to the idea? And, if so, why...?

He laughed softly. 'Ben is very definitely male. You'll see what I mean when you meet him this evening,' he responded at her questioning look. 'You surely didn't think I would be so crass as to totally upset the table arrangement by having three women and only one man?'

'I wouldn't have put it past you,' Gaye returned tartly.

But Jonathan could see her remark was only a token attempt at saving face, that Gaye was still too surprised at his friend being male and not female to be able to hide it well. She obviously hadn't liked the fact that he was bringing a woman with him. Possibly because she suspected there was more than a friendship involved in the association…?

Interesting…

And this evening promised to be even more so. Jonathan could hardly wait!

CHAPTER NINE

GAYE knew she must have checked her appearance half a dozen times as she waited for their guests to arrive!

She didn't want to appear in the least businesslike, so a blouse and skirt had been vetoed from the first, but she wasn't sure the neat black fitted dress she had finally chosen to wear, with its short length, was right either...

Her mother, when Gaye had entered the kitchen fifteen minutes earlier, had told her she looked 'beautiful'—and then promptly suggested she wear her hair loose about her shoulders rather than secured at her nape with a black slide, because she looked 'prettier' with it that way!

She had followed her mother's advice, not because she wanted to look prettier, but because she hadn't been at all sure of the severity of her hairstyle herself. But now she wondered if she looked too much as if she wanted to be found attractive!

Her nervousness about this evening wasn't helped by the fact that she was positive Jonathan had picked up this morning on her dislike of his friend apparently being female...!

She hadn't been able to help it. She was fast learning to care for Jonathan Hunter, enjoyed his company, had enjoyed those brief times she had been in his arms even more. But caring for Jonathan could be even more disastrous to her life than her feelings for Richard had turned out to be...

'This is just like old times, isn't it, darling?' her mother enthused as they put the finishing touches to the avocado and prawns they were serving as the starter to their meal, then put the elegantly prepared plates in the refrigerator to keep cool as they concentrated on the main course.

Gaye looked across at her mother now. This was the first dinner party they had given, the first time they had entertained at all, since— 'Not quite, Mummy,' she returned huskily.

Her mother returned her gaze blankly for several seconds, and then she smiled brightly. 'I'm sure it's going to be a wonderful success, darling,' she pronounced before turning her attention to the individual beef Wellingtons they had decided to cook with baby potatoes, peas and carrots. 'And I do like your Jonathan,' she added teasingly, smiling affectionately at Gaye.

She could feel the hot colour enter her cheeks. 'He isn't *my* Jonathan, Mummy,' she answered more sharply than she intended. 'He's just a friend,' she amended less tensely.

'If you say so, dear,' her mother accepted vaguely. 'Would you just like to check the table one more time to make sure we haven't forgotten anything?'

Gaye was glad of the excuse to leave the kitchen, although she knew it was completely unnecessary for her to check the dining table; her mother wouldn't have omitted anything. Gaye still found it so odd that her mother continued to function normally on every level except the part of her that refused to acknowledge the man she loved was dead...

Gaye stood in the dining room, staring sightlessly at the table. If Jonathan were to die now would she—?

No! This couldn't be happening to her! She didn't *want* this to happen to her!

But, whether she wanted it or not, she suddenly knew she had already fallen in love with Jonathan Hunter...

She sat down abruptly on one of the four chairs placed about the perfectly set table. Was she completely insane? Had she lost all her wits? Jonathan was a confirmed bachelor, if ever she had met one, and still she, with all her own scepticism about love, had fallen in love with him! It was—

'What are you doing, darling?' her mother prompted gently as she stood in the open doorway. 'The doorbell rang a minute or so ago; I thought you had gone to answer it. Are you feeling quite well, Gaye?' She frowned her concern at Gaye's continued silence.

Gaye looked at her mother for several numbed seconds—and then she deliberately shook off her feelings of disorientation. The man accompanying Jonathan might be able to help her mother; that was what was important, not her own real—or imagined—feelings for Jonathan!

'I'm fine, Mummy.' She stood up determinedly, smoothing down the skirt of her fitted dress, nevertheless showing a long expanse of shapely leg as she joined her mother in the hallway. 'Everything looks lovely.' She gave her mother an impulsive kiss on the cheek. 'Including you,' she added affectionately.

Her mother did look wonderful tonight, wearing a blue dress the exact colour of her eyes, her body full and voluptuous, but by no means fat, her legs as shapely as Gaye's, high-heeled shoes adding a little to her diminutive height. Her face was as beautifully unlined as ever, a pleased flush to her cheeks at Gaye's spontaneous

compliment, her only jewellery a pair of large gold and
sapphire earrings that glinted in the smooth blondeness
of her hair. Her mother always wore the minimum of
jewellery—'Never gild the lily', Gaye's father had always said—

Her father.

The two men waiting at the door...

'I think we had better go and let in our guests,
Mummy,' she joked even as she linked arms with her
mother, the doorbell having rung a second time—although Gaye still had no awareness of it ringing before.
Because she had been lost in thoughts of Jonathan...

It was time to bury those thoughts firmly and simply
concentrate on the evening ahead.

Although she wasn't sure that was going to be so easy
to do as she stared at Jonathan after opening the front
door!

He looked devastatingly attractive under normal circumstances, but in a black fitted evening suit and snowy
white shirt—!

Gaye felt as if all the breath had been knocked from
her body, her legs weak, her eyes wide.

The dinner suit emphasised the powerful width of
Jonathan's shoulders, his narrow waist and tapered hips,
his hair appearing more golden than ever as it brushed
the collar of the black jacket, his skin looking more
tanned too, his eyes deeply golden. He was gorgeous!

'You could have warned me, Jonathan,' drawled an
unfamiliar male voice. 'Twin visions of loveliness!'

Gaye forced her attention onto the man standing at
Jonathan's side. 'Charming' and 'very definitely male'
were the ways in which Jonathan had described his
friend Ben; the man's opening remark had proved the

former, and one only had to look at him to know the latter! Not quite as tall as Jonathan, but as powerfully built, he looked elegantly distinguished. He was probably aged in his early sixties, his hair snowy white, although this in no way detracted from his youthfully handsome face, deep blue eyes twinkling teasingly as he easily met her own.

Gaye's smile was a little shy as she looked up at him, holding out her hand. 'Mr Travis,' she greeted smoothly. 'Please, do come inside.'

'How silly of us to keep the two of you standing on the doorstep.' Her mother laughed in light dismissal as she led the way through to the lounge.

'You were worth waiting for,' the older man murmured. 'I can't tell you how much I've looked forward to meeting you,' he went on, seemingly mesmerised by Marilyn's glowing beauty.

And her mother was glowing, blushing almost girlishly at the obvious compliment.

'What a lovely thing to say,' she returned warmly. 'And do please call me Marilyn,' she invited as she moved to pour them all a glass of wine.

'It's all true too,' Jonathan said ruefully at Gaye's side. 'It seems,' he continued, the older couple out of earshot as Ben helped Marilyn with the drinks, 'that Ben has always been a Marilyn Palmer fan.' He grimaced. 'All my persuasive charm on the telephone last night was completely unnecessary; he would have paid *me* just for the chance of meeting your mother— Only a figure of speech, Gaye,' he clarified as she looked at him with surprise. 'Ben is here this evening to observe only; his fee will be the meal you give him!'

She relaxed slightly, but only slightly; she wasn't

about to let Jonathan pay any expenses. As she had already assured him, money was not a problem.

'Then let's hope he enjoys it,' she returned conversationally.

Jonathan took a light grasp of her arms, turning her to face him. 'No one is trying to step on your independent toes,' he assured her. 'Least of all me.'

She stared up at him for several long seconds, and then she sighed, forcing some of the tension out of her body. 'I'm sorry. I'm not being very grateful for all that you're trying to do. And I really do appreciate—'

'Hey.' Jonathan shook her very slightly. 'I don't believe you exactly asked for my help; it was thrust upon you.' He gave a grin. 'Your appreciation is the last thing I want.'

'Nevertheless, and no matter what happens—' she reached up on tiptoe and kissed him on the cheek '—you have it,' she told him.

'Perhaps the two of us should go out to dinner, Marilyn,' Ben Travis said as he stood across the room watching them, a glass of wine in his hand, 'and leave these two young people on their own...'

'Don't tease, Benjamin,' Marilyn reproved lightly. 'You're making Gaye blush.'

And indeed he was. Kissing Jonathan had been completely spontaneous, so much so she had completely forgotten they had an audience!

'Benjamin?' Jonathan teased very effectively diverting the attention away from Gaye.

For which she was very grateful! What on earth was she doing? Minutes ago she had been in a complete panic at the thought of loving this man, and within minutes of his arrival she had kissed him!

'I've never liked the shortening of names, Jonathan,' Gaye's mother told him as she handed him a glass. 'I have always insisted on being called by my full name of Marilyn, and I prefer to do the same with other people.'

'So that's you told, boy.' Ben gave Jonathan a hearty slap on the back. 'Marilyn prefers to call me Benjamin. What was that, Jonathan?' he persisted as Jonathan muttered something under his breath.

'Nothing of any importance,' the younger man prevaricated.

Gaye turned away to hide her smile of amusement. She had been standing closer to Jonathan than the other two, and had quite clearly heard his muttered remark: *You* would accept being called Fido by Marilyn! The thing was, Jonathan was probably quite right; her mother had always had this mesmerising effect on men. Of any age.

'What sort of work do you do, Benjamin?' Her mother skilfully changed the subject as she looked at the older man enquiringly.

Gaye instantly tensed again completely unprepared for any sort of confrontation this early in the evening. She could see by Jonathan's taut expression, as he watched the older man, that he hadn't expected this either.

But her mother was a wonderful hostess, and she had always claimed that if a person was encouraged to talk about themselves, then they would go home from the evening having enjoyed themselves. Gaye had watched her mother use this ploy over the years as she put guests at their ease. Besides, her mother was a good listener, genuinely interested in other people. And it showed.

Ben gave a lightly dismissive laugh, not appearing in

the least disconcerted by the question. 'Now, with this thatch of white hair, do I look as if I still work at anything?' He answered the question with one of his own.

'Oh, I don't know.' Gaye's mother gave him a considering look from beneath lowered lashes. 'There are so many professions nowadays that don't have a retirement age. Judges, for example.'

Ben gave a rumble of laughter. 'I can assure you I'm not—nor have I ever been—a judge.' He sobered, blue gaze suddenly very intent. 'That sort of power over the lives, or deaths, of others has never appealed to me.'

'We don't have the death sentence any more, Ben,' Jonathan told him dryly.

'Prison—any sort of prison—is a living death, Jonathan,' the older man returned harshly.

As her mother's emotional denial, self-inflicted as it seemed to be, was a prison of a kind...

Gaye looked across at Ben Travis with new eyes, seeing past the charm and distinguished good looks, noticing for the first time the deep grooves beside his mouth and nose, not put there by laughter but by pain.

She wished now that she had asked Jonathan more about the older man. She made a mental note to talk to him about Ben another time. But one thing she did know just from looking at the older man was that he had had his own share of unhappiness in his life...

'Shall we sit down?' she suggested brightly. 'We look as if we're standing in a dentist's waiting room!' She couldn't help a brief glance at Jonathan as she made the latter statement, remembering all too well how he had once castigated her concerning her formality with him— told her that she made him sound like her dentist!

'Heaven forbid!' Ben shuddered as they all sat down,

Gaye and Jonathan in armchairs, Marilyn and Ben on the three-seater sofa. 'I realise it isn't very manly to admit it—' he grimaced '—but when a dentist comes at me with that long, thin needle I just— Never mind,' he dismissed quickly, as if the mere thought of it made him cringe. 'All I meant to say is that this evening in no way compares to a visit to the dentist!' He looked across at Marilyn with open admiration.

'Let's hope you still feel that way once you've eaten!' Gaye's mother returned laughingly.

'I'm sure you cook as well as you look,' Ben said gallantly.

Jonathan gave a pained look. 'Does this approach usually work for you, Ben?' he taunted the older man affectionately.

'How should I know?' Ben gave a helpless shrug. 'It's years since I even tried! Does it work, Marilyn?' He looked at her with playful blue eyes.

She reached over and lightly touched his hand, her deeper blue eyes dancing with shared humour as she straightened. 'I have no idea, Benjamin—it's years since I tried, too! But I do find your compliments charming,' she told him warmly.

Gaye sat back and watched the older couple as they continued to talk; it was years since her mother had *tried* to be charming herself, because she had been able to beguile all around her since she was in her cradle! But Gaye had to admit it was wonderful to see her mother enjoying herself again. And she obviously was revelling in Ben's company, laughing huskily at several of his remarks, her face glowing with an inner beauty Gaye hadn't seen since— She hadn't seen her mother this happy and responsive to a man since her father was alive!

Now *there* was a complication neither she nor Jonathan had even thought of...!

Were patients allowed to fall in love with their psychiatrist? An occupational hazard, if she remembered her training correctly. But from the way Ben was staring spellbound at her mother—! Was the psychiatrist supposed to fall in love with his patient...!

The rapport between the older couple seemed to continue during the meal too, with Ben very slowly drawing her mother out to talk about her acting career. She related several amusing anecdotes, all of which included Gaye's father. Terence Royal, it quickly became obvious, was still very much alive to Marilyn...

'They seem to be getting along very well,' Jonathan said with satisfaction, having offered to go with Gaye to the kitchen to collect the cheese, which was always served before dessert in the Palmer-Royal household.

'Yes,' Gaye answered distractedly, putting the used plates from their main course into the dishwasher; to clear away as you went along was another unwritten rule in their household. A very sensible one, Gaye thought: there would be nothing worse than having to come down in the morning and clear all this away before she went to work.

Jonathan put out a hand and lifted her chin, looking down into her face, his head tilted quizzically. 'You don't seem too happy about that? Surely it's important that the two of them actually like each other?'

'Yes, of course it is. I just— They— Is Ben married?'

'What?' Jonathan released her chin, stepping back a pace.

'Don't look at me in that way, Jonathan,' Gaye protested. 'The man is halfway in love with my mother already—I think it perfectly reasonable that I want to know whether or not he's married!'

'You don't think— You aren't suggesting—'

'Jonathan, how old are you?' Gaye looked at him scathingly. 'Ben is a man—very much so, as you told me earlier today. And my mother is a very beautiful woman—'

'A woman who, in her mind at least, is still married,' he reminded her steadily.

Gaye didn't even pretend to understand the human mind, let alone explain how her mother could possibly believe her father was still alive. That wasn't a field of nursing she had chosen to specialise in, and without that specialist knowledge it could be very hard to cope with on a day-to-day basis.

'I don't think my mother's state of mind is in question, Jonathan.' She gave a sad shake of her head. 'But, from all accounts, men have been falling in love with my mother since she reached puberty. But once Mummy met and fell in love with my father she never gave any of those men so much as a second glance; they were totally, completely in love with each other. But that has never stopped others falling in love with her...' she concluded pointedly.

Jonathan looked stunned for a minute or two, scowling as her meaning sank in. Then he made a firmly dismissive gesture with his hand. 'I'm sure Ben is far too professional to allow that to happen,' he answered with certainty.

Gaye wished she could feel as sure. But Jonathan's words also confirmed that he had never fallen in love himself; it wasn't a question of allowing anything; it just happened. As her own love for him had happened...

Ben had been like a man entranced since the moment he set eyes on her mother, and while normally it wouldn't have been important... '*Is* he married, Jonathan?' The last thing any of them needed was for Ben and Marilyn's attraction to cause emotional complications in a third party's life...!

Jonathan's mouth firmed. 'He was married once. He also had a son.'

'Had?' she echoed softly.

'This is Ben's personal life, Gaye,' Jonathan told her hardly. 'Ben's son Sam was my best friend, but so is Ben. I won't betray his confidence,' he said with apology. 'It will be a different matter if he ever chooses to tell you about his wife and son himself...'

Gaye was still stunned to learn that Ben's son, and Jonathan's friend, was dead. How awful for the child to die before the parent.

She blinked back the tears. 'There's so much sadness in the world. Sometimes I understand why my mother has chosen the path she has—'

'Understand it, by all means, Gaye.' Jonathan moved, his arms curving about her waist as he drew her close to him. 'But don't ever wish you could do the same thing! It's only being half alive, Gaye—that prison Ben referred to earlier—and you, more than anyone else, must realise how awful that is for someone as vivacious as your mother!'

'She seems happy enough,' Gaye responded, her senses starting to swim.

She leant against Jonathan as if that was where she

was meant to be, her head resting under his chin, the curves of her body fitting smoothly against his.

'Rubbish,' Jonathan dismissed briskly. 'She's a bright, bubbly personality who ought to be out there in the world, warming her own and other people's lives with her charm and vitality. I realised that yesterday evening, when you came out to meet me, was probably the first time you had been out socially in a very long time. But how long is it since Marilyn went out for an evening, met friends?'

He was right; of course he was. After all, wasn't that why they were all here?

'You're right,' she agreed, allowing herself the sheer luxury of being held close to him for a few more seconds before forcing herself to move away. 'Let's take in the cheese—before they send out a search party for us! Maybe I was overreacting just now concerning Ben's friendliness towards my mother. It would have been awful if he were rude to her and she ended up hating him!'

Although she didn't feel quite as confident a few minutes later when they rejoined the other couple in the dining room and her mother happily announced that Ben had invited her out to dinner—and she had accepted!

CHAPTER TEN

'I'M SURE you know what you're doing, Ben.' Jonathan glanced at the man seated beside him in the car as he drove the two of them home from dinner. 'But I'm damned if I do,' he added grimly.

He had felt such a fool, convincing Gaye in the kitchen that Ben was a complete professional when it came to his work, only to return to the dining room and be greeted with the fact that the other couple intended going out to dinner together. And that feeling wasn't lessened by Gaye's 'I told you so' look!

Ben barely glanced at him, completely relaxed in the passenger seat. 'You'll just have to trust me, Jonathan, that I know exactly what I'm doing. God, but she's a beautiful woman, isn't she?' he said admiringly.

Much as Jonathan considered Gaye the most beautiful woman he had ever seen, he knew very well his friend wasn't talking about her!

'I've seen every one of her films, you know,' Ben continued warmly. 'And she's electric on stage!'

'I know,' Jonathan acknowledged dryly. 'I've seen her several times myself. I couldn't believe it when I actually met her last night. But Gaye is—concerned—'

'Hmm—Gaye,' Ben echoed slowly, turning to give Jonathan a considering look. 'When we talked last night you didn't mention that the two of you are—'

'Because we're not!' Jonathan cut in flatly, picking up all too easily on the implication in the other man's tone.

118

'Keep working on it, Jonathan,' Ben chuckled. 'And you will be!'

He stiffened in his seat, his hands tightening on the steering-wheel. Something else that had gone slightly wrong with this evening was that when he'd offered to drive Ben to dinner he hadn't taken into account that he would also have to drive the other man home again, totally preventing himself from spending any time alone with Gaye to say goodnight. He had had to be satisfied with those few moments they had spent together in the kitchen when he had at least managed to hold her, having no choice but to merely kiss her and her mother on the cheek before leaving a few minutes ago.

'I would rather not discuss Gaye in those terms,' he bit out abruptly, his expression grim.

'Oh?' Ben raised snowy white brows.

'Yes—oh,' Jonathan confirmed tightly.

Ben settled himself more comfortably in his seat. 'Does this mean I'm shortly to be invited to another Hunter wedding?' he drawled teasingly. 'After years of bachelorhood, you're starting to drop like flies—'

'I am *not* going to marry Gaye,' Jonathan finally managed to interrupt tautly, having briefly—very briefly—been rendered speechless at the mention of the word 'wedding'!

'No?' Ben said sceptically.

'Despite Jarrett's marriage, not all the Hunter brothers have taken leave of their senses,' he dismissed scornfully. 'You're as likely to marry Marilyn Palmer as *I* am to marry her daughter!'

'You're well aware of my views on marriage, boy,' Ben replied.

'Exactly,' Jonathan acknowledged with satisfaction. 'More or less a match for my own!'

'Nevertheless,' Ben said slowly, 'Gaye is a very lovely young woman.'

Jonathan stiffened. 'There are millions of lovely young women in the world, Ben,' he said.

'Probably,' the older man conceded dryly. 'But very few of them have that unique combination of beauty, vulnerability and fierce independence that Gaye possesses. Do you know who she reminds me of...?'

'I thought you said she was unique?' Jonathan was deliberately challenging, sure he wasn't going to like the answer to Ben's question.

Ben nodded. 'Oh, but she is. As unique as Abbie...' he decided.

Jonathan's mouth clamped shut, his teeth grinding together. He knew exactly what Ben was doing. He and Jordan both thought the world of Abbie, couldn't have loved her more if she had really been their sister, both of them answering any teasing about their own unmarried state with the reply that they would only marry if they could find someone as beautiful and caring as Abbie!

Ben was right; Gaye was all of those things...

Jonathan knew he was quiet during lunch the next day. Also knew that Gaye was aware of it, as she listened attentively to what Ben had to say about her mother.

Jonathan told himself he was staying out of the conversation because Gaye only had an hour for lunch, and what Ben had to say to her was more important than anything he might have been able to add to the conversation.

He told himself that, but he knew he was lying...

As much as he wished he could deny it, he knew that what Ben had said to him the previous evening had struck a raw nerve. Was he falling in love with Gaye? Or was it already too late, and he was in love with her?

He watched her now as she listened so intently to Ben, those beautiful deep green eyes glowing with interest, her mouth curving almost into a smile, the lower lip full and sensuous. And her hair—! She was wearing it loose about her shoulders again today, and Jonathan wanted nothing more than to bury his hands in its silkiness while he took possession of that invitingly sensual mouth!

Was it too late?

She had interested him from the first, challenged him, aroused him—and she still did! But he didn't want to fall in love with any woman, couldn't—

'—up to you and Jonathan?' Ben looked at the two of them enquiringly, drawing Jonathan back into the conversation—a conversation he hadn't been listening to!

Gaye looked at him too, anxiously, and Jonathan wondered exactly what it was he had missed. This wasn't like him, his mind always able to function on several levels at the same time. But not, it seemed, when Gaye was around...

Pull yourself together, man, he inwardly chided himself. 'Sorry?' He looked at the other man questioningly.

'I think the answer to that has to be no, Ben,' Gaye told the psychiatrist, deliberately, Jonathan felt, not meeting his own gaze. 'It isn't necessary for me to play chaperon when you and my mother go out tomorrow evening,' she said. 'And I've already taken up far too much of Jonathan's time with my family business,' she finished distantly.

What he had missed, it now became apparent to Jonathan, was Ben's suggestion that he and Gaye accompany the older couple tomorrow evening when they went out to dinner. And he had shown so much enthusiasm for the idea, he hadn't even heard the suggestion! No wonder Gaye had chosen to turn down the idea for both of them!

Or was it something else that had made her turn down the invitation? Had she heard from Craven again? He had been far too busy these last thirty-six hours to contact the man himself, but he had made a mental note to do so at the earliest opportunity, probably later this afternoon; Jarrett was taking Abbie and the baby home today, and Jordan was more than capable of holding the Hunter fort alone...

'Dinner tomorrow evening sounds a good idea to me,' he told Ben harshly, golden gaze defiant as he looked at Gaye. If she said she had other plans—

'I'll book the table for four,' Ben put in smoothly before Gaye could say anything, glancing at his slim gold watch. 'Now I believe it's time for you to go back to work, young lady,' he told Gaye lightly. 'I could drive you—'

'I have something else I need to discuss with Gaye,' Jonathan cut in. 'And we can do that on the drive back to the clinic,' he added firmly, watching as Gaye obviously had an inner struggle as to whether or not this was one of those fights that needed fighting! He couldn't exactly blame her; he was behaving extremely arrogantly. 'Please,' he added tautly, having had the definite feeling that Gaye was about to lose this particular struggle.

Ben grinned as he stood up to leave, obviously enjoying Jonathan's discomfort, even going so far as to wink across at him. 'My mother always told me that you catch more with honey than with vinegar, Jonathan,' he taunted.

Jonathan glowered up at Ben. 'Your mother was a—'

'Charming and lovely woman,' Ben finished for him. 'And I won't have a word said against her. I'll look forward to seeing you again tomorrow evening, my dear.' He bent and gave Gaye a perfunctory kiss on the cheek, openly laughing as he looked across at Jonathan. 'Would you like to drive tomorrow evening, or shall I?'

Damn the man; he even knew of Jonathan's inner frustration about last night! 'I suggest we both drive. I'm sure Gaye and I have no wish to cramp your style,' he responded with soft derision.

'Or I yours,' Ben returned unabashedly, lifting a hand in parting, wending his way easily between the tables, despite his considerable size.

He left complete silence behind him. Gaye, Jonathan was sure, still hadn't completely won her inward struggle, and he knew that struggle was his fault; he had behaved boorishly, so it was no wonder Gaye didn't want to spend tomorrow evening in his company too!

'Sorry,' he sighed apologetically. 'I haven't been very good company today,' he continued at her questioning look, knowing it was his behaviour that had also put that pained look in those beautiful green eyes. He reached over and lightly clasped her hand as it rested on the table-top. 'It started out with me leaving you and Ben to discuss what needed to be discussed, and then—well, I just lost it. I was miles away in thought when the suggestion for dinner came up. I—'

'You're a busy man, Jonathan,' Gaye said quietly, looking down to where his hand clasped hers rather than into his face. 'I'm very grateful for the time you've already given to this. I don't want to take up—'

'This sounds suspiciously like a dismissal to me,' he cut in.

'Of course not,' she protested, her startled gaze rising to meet his. 'I just don't want to be responsible for taking advantage of your kindness—'

'I'll let you know when you've taken advantage, Gaye,' he assured her. He should be so lucky! 'Tomorrow night is all settled. Now let's go and sort out a provisional driving licence for you.' He pulled her to her feet, keeping hold of her hand as they made their way out of the restaurant.

Gaye looked up at him once they were outside on the pavement. 'Was that the something else you wanted to talk to me about?'

From the relief he could read in that candid green gaze, he had a feeling she had thought it was something else entirely that he had wanted to talk to her about! But what? From the guard that suddenly fell over her eyes he knew she wasn't about to tell him.

'It was.' He nodded in confirmation.

She looked embarrassed now, moistening her lips with the tip of her tongue. 'I—' She swallowed hard. 'I've already taken care of it,' she admitted reluctantly. 'Well, you did offer to teach me,' she rushed on as he raised surprised brows. 'And so I—'

'It's all right, Gaye.' He cut her off by giving her a hug, suddenly feeling light-hearted, as if a heavy weight had been lifted off his shoulders.

Gaye wasn't reluctant to see him again; in fact she

had taken a step that would ensure that she did. And he was glad. So pleased he could have shouted his pleasure out loud.

But what sense this made of his terror during lunch, when he had considered the possibility of falling in love with this woman, he didn't know. However, for the moment, he didn't care!

'Of course I'll teach you to drive. Now I had better get you back to the clinic.' He held her arm lightly as he opened the car door for her, grinning as she gave him a confused glance before slowly getting into the passenger seat.

She was confused?

She should try being inside *his* head!

Jonathan looked at Richard Craven with unconcealed dislike. The other man was still good-looking, still powerfully built, but in the cold light of afternoon those lines of dissipation were more evident, and without the charm of his smile his face possessed a definite arrogance. Arrogance he attempted to use to full effect as he returned Jonathan's scathing stare with one of venomous dislike.

'To what do I owe this pleasure?' Richard drawled in carefully measured tones. 'It must be something important for you to have taken the trouble to find me in this way,' he added with satisfaction, the blue eyes not full of humour today but filled with a hardness Jonathan knew he could more than match.

But could Gaye...?

Jonathan's mouth tightened as he thought of what Gaye had suffered at this man's ruthless hands. 'I can assure you,' he replied hardly, 'the pleasure is all yours!

And it was no trouble at all to find you; my cousin is
Gabriel Hunter.' His expression was deliberately bland
as he calmly looked at the younger man and watched
the information he had just imparted slowly sink in.

And sink in it did, and not so slowly either. They were
seated slightly away from the set of the film Richard
Craven was currently starring in, and the other man had
been lounging back in his chair seconds earlier, his feet
up on a table, but at the mention of Gabe's name his
feet suddenly hit the floor as he sat forward on the edge
of his seat.

'Who the hell are you?' he demanded to know vi-
ciously.

Jonathan shrugged. 'I just told you, Gabe Hunter's
cousin.' As a film and theatre critic, Gabe had been
known to make or break an actor's or actress's career.
One phone call to his cousin and Jonathan had learnt
exactly where Richard Craven could be found. Within
an hour of making that call, he had been confronting the
man himself.

'And exactly what are you to Gaye?' Most of the
sneering arrogance had gone now, but a certain defiance
still remained.

Jonathan met the other man's gaze unblinkingly. 'I'm
a family friend,' he told him pointedly. 'Do I make myself clear?' There was a steely edge to his voice now.

Richard made a casual gesture. 'I was only—'

'Let me make myself clearer,' Jonathan continued
icily. 'I have already advised you to stay away from
Gaye and Marilyn, but let me add something to that. The
next time it won't be advice. And it won't be via the
telephone.'

'Yes,' the other man drawled, with only a little of his earlier bravado, 'you *are* Gabe's cousin!'

Jonathan smiled as he stood up to leave, but it was a smile that didn't reach his eyes. 'I'm glad we understand each other.' He made to leave.

'Is Gaye in love with you?'

He stiffened, turning slowly back to face the other man, brows arched. 'Is that any of your business?'

'I suppose not,' Richard conceded. 'I just wondered if she was happy...'

Jonathan's eyes narrowed. There was an element of something in the other man's voice that he didn't like, a—a caring, possibly. And he felt his chest constrict at the thought of him having once loved Gaye. And of her having returned that love...

'She's happy,' he told Richard flatly.

The actor nodded, that fleeting something—whatever it had been!—now gone, as he gave a taunting smile. 'I don't envy you,' he scorned. 'Gaye is a cold little fish. And as Marilyn Palmer, world-renowned actress, her mother would have made a wonderful mother-in-law, but what she is now...'

Jonathan moved so fast Richard didn't even see him coming! But as Jonathan grabbed Richard by the shirt-front and pulled him to his feet, his face barely inches away from the other man's, he knew he had Richard's complete attention.

'She's *still* Marilyn Palmer, Craven. She will *always* be Marilyn Palmer. And as for Gaye...' He threw the other man back into his chair before he had a chance to give in to the impulse he had to smack that sneering smile off the other man's too good-looking face. 'You obviously weren't the right man for her. I find her warm, responsive, absolutely beautiful.' In his arms that was exactly what she was!

Richard seemed unfazed. 'But will that last?' He was deliberately scathing.

'With me?' Jonathan grated. 'Absolutely.'

He drew in several deep breaths of fresh air once he reached his car, somehow feeling as if he hadn't breathed properly for some time. He also felt, after being near the other man, that he needed a shower, to wash Richard Craven's slime off him; he had never met a man he disliked that intensely. Never met *anyone* he disliked as much as he disliked Richard Craven!

But could the other man's description of Gaye being cold possibly mean what he was beginning to hope that it did? Had Gaye never known the pleasure and joy of physical love? Not with Craven, that was for sure. And the last two years she hadn't had any boyfriends, because she had concentrated solely on her mother...

But in his arms she was warm and responsive, shyly matching his passion, was everything any man could ever want or need. She was, he now felt certain, completely untouched...

He felt his senses stir just at the thought of seeing her again.

But he didn't feel quite so elated when he arrived at Gaye's home the next evening to pick her up for dinner, and discovered a huge arrangement of flowers in the hallway, the card with them reading 'From your biggest fan, Richard!'

He should have punched the other man on the nose when he'd had the chance!

CHAPTER ELEVEN

GAYE watched in dismay as Jonathan's smile of greeting faded to be replaced by a dark scowl as he looked at the bouquet of yellow and cream roses.

'He sent them to my mother earlier today,' she explained awkwardly. 'She thinks they're beautiful. A charming gesture, from a charming man. And I didn't know how to—'

'Your mother?' Jonathan bit out abruptly, looking at her blankly now. 'Craven sent the flowers to *your* mother?'

'Yes.' Gaye picked out the card, turning it over to reveal more of the large scrawl. 'He says he's sorry they won't be working together after all.' She read out the message on the back of the card before putting it back amongst the roses. 'I don't know what changed his mind about that, I'm just grateful that he has!'

What was wrong with Jonathan? She had been looking forward to seeing him all day, and she had seen the admiration light up his eyes a few minutes ago when she'd opened the door to him and he'd taken in her appearance and her fitted green dress, its short length showing off her legs. But as soon as he had walked into the hallway his attitude had changed!

In fact, he seemed to be acting very strangely altogether at the moment! He had appeared fine the other evening, when he and Ben were here for dinner, but at lunch yesterday—! She wasn't even sure why he had

129

bothered to join them; he had certainly added little to the conversation, and his glowering behaviour had been decidedly unnerving. She wasn't sure, from what she had already seen of him, that this evening was going to be any better...

'How are Abbie and Conor?' she asked conversationally as they went through to the sitting room to join her mother and Ben, her mother looking lovely in a black dress that showed her voluptuous figure to advantage, Ben once again distinguished in black evening suit and snowy white shirt.

Gaye's interest in Abbie and Conor wasn't merely polite. She genuinely missed the other woman's warm friendliness, and it seemed quite empty at the clinic now without Abbie's fun personality. Also, Gaye had to inwardly acknowledge, Abbie had taken with her the chance of any of the Hunter brothers putting in an appearance...

Jonathan hadn't just crept into her life, he had invaded it with the force of a tidal wave, seemingly leaving her no choice but to follow along in its wake. Which was one of the reasons she had taken it upon herself to organise her own driving licence. He might—or might not—have decided to teach her to drive, but she was certainly old enough, and capable enough, to organise the rest of it for herself!

'Jarrett is clucking over both of them like a mother hen with her two chicks.' Jonathan dryly answered her question, smiling. 'With Charlie as his more than willing accomplice! I give Abbie two days at the most before she very politely but firmly tells them both to go away! Evening, Ben, Marilyn,' he greeted the other couple, bending low to kiss Marilyn warmly on the cheek.

Something he certainly hadn't done to Gaye when he arrived!

Her mother smiled her pleasure at seeing him again. 'Is it polite to ask who Jarrett, Abbie and Conor are?' she enquired lightly. 'And Charlie too, of course.'

Gaye had told her mother very little about Jonathan, and certainly nothing about his family; it wouldn't do for her mother to jump to any conclusions! But she listened with amusement as Jonathan described his older brother as a slave-driver, Jarrett's beautiful wife Abbie as having the patience of Job, the merits of their new-born son, and the endearingly lovely Charlie. Jordan he described as an irrepressible torment.

'Don't deprecate such an enchanting-sounding family, Jonathan,' Gaye's mother told him softly. 'I know that Terence and I always wanted—' She broke off, looking confused for a moment. But only for a moment. 'We were always sorry we weren't able to give Gaye a brother or a sister,' she continued lightly. 'It would have been so much nicer for Gaye if we had. Do you have children, Benjamin?'

Gaye's breath suddenly caught in her throat—and held. Ben had a son. But he had died. She glanced uncertainly at Jonathan, but his gaze was fixed intently on Ben.

'I had a son, Marilyn,' Ben replied without hesitation, his eyes direct and sure on Marilyn's face. 'Unfortunately, he was born with a heart defect. I won't bore you with all the details,' he said, 'but after several operations he was able to lead a more or less normal life. It was all a bit too much for his mother. She wasn't able to accept that he wasn't perfect, and when Sam was three she left us.'

'Oh, Benjamin…' Gaye's mother groaned. 'How awful for you both! But—but you said your son had—died.' The last word was forced out of her, her eyes wide purple smudges in the paleness of her face.

Ben nodded. 'Sam lived a quieter life than most children, but, I believe, a happy one—'

'Very,' Jonathan put in softly. 'Sam was my best friend,' he explained to Marilyn.

Pain. Both men showed real pain in talking about the young man they had obviously both cared for very much.

Gaye looked worriedly at her mother. Although she knew exactly what Ben was doing. He had discussed this with her yesterday at lunch. Her mother, over the last two years, living the way that she had, had managed to shut out all emotional pain. Anything unpleasant, or painful, she shied away from. Without actually subjecting Marilyn to her own personal grief, Ben intended gradually introducing her to the emotion she refused to face—pain. But Gaye had had no idea that he intended doing so by exposing his own emotional loss!

Ben nodded his gratitude at Jonathan's reassurance. 'Like a lot of children with a physical disability, Sam had a wonderful mind. At twenty-two, he had just completed a Masters degree, was about to begin a Ph.D., when he was senselessly knocked over and killed by a speeding car.'

He revealed the last without bitterness or accusation, merely stated what had happened. But the effect on Gaye's mother was momentarily devastating, her beautiful face crumpling with grief, eyes dark violet shadows.

But it was only a momentary break in her composure; her expression became sad now, full of sympathy, almost making Gaye imagine that look of devastation seconds ago. Almost...

'I'm so sorry, Benjamin.' Marilyn touched his arm. 'I can't even begin to imagine what it must be like to lose your child.'

'Let's hope you never have to.' Ben squeezed her hand before turning to Gaye and Jonathan. 'Time we were leaving, I think, don't you?' he prompted, the smile back on his lips, although not quite back in his eyes.

'He reached her for a moment, didn't he?' Jonathan said evenly as he and Gaye travelled to the restaurant in his car, her mother in the following Mercedes with Ben.

Gaye glanced at Jonathan, still unsure of his mood. He seemed strange today, somehow distant, and she wasn't sure how to respond to him. Teasing or arrogant she could deal with; distant was something else entirely!

'Yes, I think he did.' She knew exactly what he was referring to. 'I'm so sorry about your friend, Jonathan. And Ben...' She bit her bottom lip. 'Like my mother, I can't imagine what it must have been like for him.' She spoke in an unsteady voice.

'Sam was his life,' Jonathan said tonelessly. 'After his wife walked out on them Ben became mother as well as father to Sam. I only met Sam when I went to university, but Sam had nothing but admiration for his father, and the bond between the two of them was—well, it was like nothing I've ever seen between father and son. It almost killed Ben too when Sam died so senselessly. His hair turned white overnight, it seemed, and for months no one could reach him. What saved him was other people like your mother, I think, people who had suffered a loss that was just too big for them to take on board. Helping those people come to terms with their own private hell was what saved Ben's own sanity.' He glanced briefly at Gaye. 'I'm not sure, in the same circumstances, that I could have done what he does.'

'No,' Gaye agreed quietly. Because each time Ben helped someone else with their grief he had to suffer through his own all over again...!

'Have I told you yet this evening how beautiful you're looking?'

She looked suddenly across at Jonathan, as much for his flirtatious tone as for what he'd actually said. Maybe this evening wasn't going to be a repeat of lunch yesterday, after all...

'No,' she answered vivaciously.

'You look lovely.' He grinned at her. 'But then, you always do!'

'Always?' She arched her brows. 'I think hospital theatre gowns leave a lot to be desired!' She teasingly reminded him of the first time they met.

'Well, I must admit, I like the green dress you're wearing this evening much better,' he returned dryly.

Gaye felt her own mood lighten to match his. Thank goodness! She had felt the tension between them the last thirty-six hours, and been uncomfortable with it. Although she wasn't even sure Jonathan was aware of it...

It turned out to be a fun evening, those few brief minutes of emotional awareness at the house, when Ben talked of his son's death, put firmly in the background. By Ben too. Gaye had to admire the way he could do that. It couldn't have been easy for him to talk about his son's life, and death, so candidly, and yet, Gaye realised, it was the way he got through to the people he helped. He knew the trauma his patients had suffered, related to it completely, and by making those patients aware of that he was gradually able to break through their barriers. There could never be any accusations of his not understanding.

They ate in a quietly exclusive restaurant, where it was obvious that several other diners recognised Gaye's mother, but were too polite to come and interrupt her evening out with friends. The food was excellent, the service discreet, the company faultless; as her mother's first social outing for some time, Gaye didn't think it could have been bettered.

She told Jonathan of her pleasure in the evening as he drove her home some time later. 'My mother sparkled tonight, as she used to,' she said excitedly. 'Daddy always said my mother responded to an audience,' she recalled affectionately.

He nodded. 'She really should return to acting. Oh, not with Craven,' he added darkly. 'The further you both stay away from *him* the better.' He scowled. 'But your father was right; your mother needs an audience. It enables her to blossom and glow. I'm sure she enjoyed her evening.'

There had only been one awkward moment during dinner. And once again it had been Jonathan's rapid change of mood that had caused it. Gaye and her mother had disappeared to the ladies' room before coffee was served, and the two men were sitting at the table talking when they returned, a conversation that ended as soon as the two women came within earshot. But, whatever their discussion had been about, it had far from pleased Jonathan—whereas Ben had looked amused by the whole thing.

Jonathan's mood hadn't really lifted again after that,

although it had in no way hindered her mother's obvious enjoyment of the evening, which was, after all, the purpose of it taking place at all. The other couple were still chatting warmly together when Jonathan had suddenly suggested driving Gaye home. But, all in all, Gaye still thought the evening a success...

Although she had a feeling Jonathan was beginning to wish he had never become involved...

'Thank you for introducing Ben to us,' Gaye told him as he stopped the car in the driveway. 'I think—I have a feeling he really is going to be able to help.' It was the first sense of optimism she had had for a very long time.

Jonathan switched off the engine, turning to her in the darkness. 'I'm sure he is. But why do I have the feeling that remark was something of a goodbye...?' He quirked blond brows.

She felt the warmth in her cheeks. It had probably felt like a goodbye because it was one. He had spent far too much of his time already on helping her with her problems; she certainly wasn't going to keep him to his offer to teach her to drive. His erratic mood of the last two days spoke of an impatience with the whole situation.

'We've taken up so much of your time already this last week—'

'Gaye, let me assure you, I never do anything I don't want to do,' he said forcefully.

Her eyes widened incredulously. 'Never?'

'No, never. And do you know what I want to do right now?'

Her eyes had adjusted to the semi-darkness now, and as she looked at his intense expression she knew exactly what he wanted to do! She felt herself tense expectantly.

'Don't say you don't know,' he husked as he reached out and drew her towards him. 'Although I have to admit I think I'm a little old to be caught kissing a girl in my car—even if it is on the front seat and not the back!'

Gaye gazed up at him, her breath catching in her throat; Jonathan intended kissing her! And she wanted him to. More than anything! 'If you would rather, we could always go into the house,' she offered.

He straightened. 'I would rather.'

Gaye felt self-conscious as she unlocked the door and let them both into the house. What was she doing? Inviting him in was tantamount to asking to be kissed. Not that she didn't want to be kissed—she just wished she hadn't made it so obvious!

'Stop thinking so much,' Jonathan murmured indulgently as they walked into the sitting room, putting a gentle hand under her chin to tilt her face up to his. 'It gives you frown-lines, right here.' He bent and gently kissed her between the eyes. 'And I can assure you,' he added thickly, 'you have only gone up in my estimation, not down, because you're a woman who prefers being made love to in private.'

She gave him a startled look. She wanted to be kissed; making love was something else entirely!

But as Jonathan's mouth possessively claimed hers there was no time to protest. And as the kiss deepened with passion she found she didn't want to protest, her arms moving up over his shoulders as he moulded her body against the hardness of his.

A side lamp had been left on to illuminate the room while they were out, but the shadows it cast only added to the intimacy of the situation, Jonathan settling them both on the length of the sofa, his gaze deeply golden as he looked down into Gaye's face.

'Beautiful,' he said gruffly, before his head lowered and his lips once more claimed hers.

Gaye felt her senses soar, lost in the warmth and totally male smell of him, his shoulders and back so firm to her touch, one of his legs lying across both of hers. She almost felt like a part of him. Almost...

His lips were against her throat now, the top of her breasts revealed by the low neckline of her dress, his hands restlessly caressing her hips and thighs. As if he didn't think they were close enough either!

Jonathan shrugged out of his jacket, murmuring softly as his lips sought and found the creaminess of her breasts, fingers lightly caressing one already hardened tip, the pleasure of that touch filling Gaye with a heady warmth.

But she still wanted more, so much more, and she knew by the hard contours of Jonathan's body that he felt that same need.

She arched back in pleasure as the warmth of his mouth claimed the rosy tip of her breast, his tongue weaving a magic all of its own as he ran its moistness over that hardened nub.

Gaye felt warm, hot, on fire, her thighs moving restlessly against his, wanting—wanting—

'Gaye, I want you!' Jonathan groaned as he laid his head on the nakedness of her breasts. 'But your mother and Ben could return at any moment—'

'I forgot...!' she groaned. She had forgotten everything but Jonathan these last few minutes, and even now, as she looked at him in the semi-darkness, she liked the feel of his head against her breasts, his hair soft and silky, his breath warm against her skin, his hands sensitive as he lightly caressed her arm. 'We can't let them find us like this,' she agreed unsteadily, unable to hide her own regret at the inappropriateness of where they were.

Jonathan gave a shuddering sigh as he moved away from her, turning away to sit up beside where she still lay, his face buried briefly in his hands.

Gaye appreciated those few moments to collect her scattered wits together. And also to put her dress back in place! Somewhere during their lovemaking Jonathan had pulled the zip down at its back, enabling him to push the material out of the way of his questing hands and lips.

He turned as Gaye was struggling to pull up the zip. 'Here, let me.' He turned her slightly, easily pulling the fastener back into place. 'There.' He gently smoothed back her tangled hair. 'Now no one need ever know.'

Gaye knew... And she didn't think she would ever forget, could still feel the caress of his hands, that velvet tongue as he—

'No,' she agreed softly, swinging her legs down onto the floor. And just in time, it seemed, as she heard the front door open and her mother laugh at something Ben had just said to her.

As the older couple seemed to take an age to come through to the lounge, Gaye had the sinking feeling that the remark had something to do with Jonathan and herself. Her cheeks burned with embarrassment as she realised her mother and Ben had probably guessed exactly what they were interrupting! Was her attraction towards Jonathan that obvious?

She stood up abruptly, moving away from where

Jonathan still sat on the sofa, pulling his jacket back on now, although his movements were unhurried. Gaye couldn't even look at him, her cheeks pale now.

Jonathan stood up too as the older couple came into the room. 'Just in time,' he told them smoothly, the grimness of his expression not reflected in the lightness of his tone. 'I was just about to leave.'

That was certainly news to Gaye; until a few minutes ago he had given every impression that he wanted to stay. For the night, at least!

Ben looked at the younger man knowingly. 'Marilyn was just about to make some coffee,' he said slowly.

'Not for me, I'm afraid.' Jonathan smiled to take the sting out of his refusal.

At least, he smiled at Gaye's mother... He seemed to be avoiding looking at Gaye as much as she was avoiding looking at him!

'I have an early appointment tomorrow,' he continued, 'so I have to be bright and alert in the morning. No, don't bother to see me to the door, Gaye,' he said as she moved to do just that. 'I can see myself out. Thank you all for an enjoyable evening,' he added politely.

But it was only a politeness; he was already on his way out of the door as he said it. As if he couldn't wait to get away...

And he went, without even telling Gaye when—or indeed if—he would be seeing her again!

CHAPTER TWELVE

JONATHAN was running scared, and he knew it.

And it was all Ben's fault, damn him!

He had felt he'd recovered quite well from arriving at Gaye's to find those flowers from Richard Craven in the hallway, although his relief had been immense when he had realised they had been sent to Marilyn and not Gaye, and that Richard had apparently decided not to direct Marilyn in his play. Yes, he had recovered well, had been able to talk quite normally to Gaye in the car on the way to the restaurant, the meal itself progressing very successfully—until Ben had made an announcement that had so totally thrown him, he had felt as if someone had punched him in the chest!

The two ladies had just disappeared to the powder room before they all had coffee, when Ben had turned to him and calmly told him to get out his morning suit—because once Marilyn was able to cope with the idea he intended marrying her!

The look that had accompanied the statement was clearly meant to remind Jonathan of his earlier claim of being as likely to marry Gaye as Ben was to marry Marilyn...! It had been obvious from the seriousness of his expression that Ben had really meant what he had said!

Jonathan had known Ben for years, had continued his friendship with him after Sam's death, and he had never seen the other man seriously interested in any woman,

Ben having been soured against the marital state by the failure of his previous marriage. But Jonathan didn't doubt that he meant what he said about marrying Marilyn...

Somehow Jonathan felt as if people he had thought he knew—first Jarrett had fallen in love with Abbie, and now Ben had fallen for Marilyn—were no longer who or what he had thought they were. In all honesty, he was worried the same thing might happen to him. Worried. And then upset. And, he admitted with self-reproach, downright angry. He had taken Gaye home and made love to her in that frame of mind!

He could never remember feeling like this in his life before, was almost ashamed of his own actions, but at the same time having no intention of apologising for them. Because if he apologised he would have to explain why—and that was definitely something he didn't want to do!

If only he didn't feel constantly haunted by a pair of hurt green eyes...

'Is it safe to come in?' Jarrett paused next to the office door he had just opened without knocking. 'Only Trish tells me you're a little—on edge today.' He strolled into the room without invitation, closing the door behind him.

Trish had been Jonathan's secretary for the last ten years; aged in her mid-fifties, she tended to mother him—and Jonathan very much doubted she had used the words 'on edge' to describe his mood lately!

'Why aren't you at home with your wife and son?' Jonathan returned irritably; Jarrett had barely been to the office at all since Conor's birth just over a week ago.

'Yep.' Jarrett gave a satisfied nod as he gave Jonathan a considering look. 'On edge.'

'I am not—' Jonathan broke off, drawing in a deeply controlling breath. 'How's the family?'

His older brother sat on the side of his desk, golden gaze thoughtful. 'Why don't you come for dinner this evening and see for yourself?'

'Abbie has enough to do without entertaining me,' Jonathan replied dismissively.

Jarrett's mouth twisted. 'I have no intention of Abbie 'entertaining' you,' he drawled mockingly. 'But she did mention at breakfast this morning that we haven't seen much of you the last few days.'

Jonathan wasn't fooled for a moment by the casualness of the remark, fingers tightly gripping the pen he had been writing with—or, at least, trying to write with; he didn't seem able to concentrate recently. 'I've been busy,' he bit out tautly.

Jarrett nodded. 'I can imagine,' he said. 'Abbie suggested you bring Gaye along to dinner this evening—'

'Then I suggest Abbie asks her—and leaves me out of it!' Jonathan stood up restlessly, turning to look out of his window at the London rooftops. 'Gaye's a big girl; I'm sure she's quite capable of bringing herself to dinner.' By bus, or taxi, because she couldn't drive herself there, and he had no intention of teaching her to drive any more, either...

'Have the two of you argued?'

Jonathan rounded on Jarrett. 'No, we damn well haven't—' Again he drew in a deeply controlling breath, avoiding meeting Jarrett's searching gaze. His older brother was far too astute for anyone's good... But the last thing he wanted was for Gaye and himself to be considered a couple. He was a free agent—and intended remaining that way! 'I have been helping Gaye with a personal—damn it, you know what I've been helping her with!' he rasped. 'But Ben now has that situation under control.' To such an extent, he intended marrying his patient!

Jarrett quirked his brows. 'And you?'

He didn't have anything under control; that was his problem! 'Ben doesn't need my help any more,' he shrugged.

'What about Gaye?' Jarrett prompted softly.

'Damn it—what about her?' he exploded impatiently, moving forcefully. 'I've taken an interest in a woman before—'

'Dozens of them,' his brother conceded.

'Exactly,' Jonathan snapped. 'I don't remember any of these matchmaking tactics with them.' He glared fiercely.

Jarrett looked amused. 'We didn't meet most of them, and the few that we did—!'

Jonathan could feel himself becoming flushed with annoyance. 'They weren't that bad, damn it,' he barked. 'I met Gaye, I liked her, she had a problem, I've done what I can to help resolve that problem; there's no reason for me to see her again.'

Except that he had missed her the last couple of days, missed her beauty, that quiet charm, the tinkling sound of her laughter...

'Does there have to be a reason?' Jarrett asked quietly, watching him with narrowed eyes.

Jonathan gave a heavy sigh. 'I don't want to get involved, Jarrett—'

'You're already involved, Jonathan,' his brother put in gently.

He gave a firm shake of his head. 'I've made myself *un*involved. And I'm going to stay that way,' he added grimly. 'Thank Abbie for the dinner invitation, but I already have a date this evening.' With the female friend he should have met earlier in the week. Sarah was a model, beautiful, independent, with no interest in a permanent relationship. An evening spent in her effervescent company—better yet, a night in her bed—and he would have forgotten all about Gaye Royal. He hoped.

Jarrett stood up to leave. 'Abbie is going to be disappointed.'

'I'll come round tomorrow to make up for it!'

'Make sure that you do.'

Jonathan moved back to sit behind his desk once Jarrett had gone from his office. Much as he loved Abbie, and Jarrett, and, of course, the two children, he was not in the mood to play happy families at the moment! Jarrett might be happily married, but as all the brothers knew only too well not all marriages were like his—in fact most of them weren't. Their parents certainly hadn't been. Jarrett had just been lucky. Besides, Jonathan had no inclination to settle down in a relationship with one woman.

Even if she did have haunting green eyes...

Maybe if Gaye herself had been different, then the whole situation would have been different too. But from what Richard Craven had implied about his own relationship with Gaye Jonathan had a feeling they hadn't had a physical relationship. And if she hadn't had a physical relationship with the man she'd intended marrying...! He had been elated about that at first, but now

it scared the hell out of him. Gaye was a woman who
would settle for nothing less than marriage.

She wasn't for him!

Sarah was much more his type...

What a disastrous evening!

Mainly his own fault, Jonathan had to admit. Sarah
had been her usually bubbly self, had a party for the two
of them to go to. Ordinarily Jonathan would have enjoyed the party, knowing a lot of Sarah's friends already,
all of them intent on having a good time. Jonathan had
felt like the only teetotaller in a wine-tasting evening—
totally alone, and slightly removed from the whole thing!

Sarah had been quick to notice his lack of enthusiasm
for their surroundings, suggesting the two of them leave
after only being there an hour. But Jonathan had felt that
was unfair on Sarah; she worked hard, but she liked to
play hard too, and he'd known he was the one putting a
dampener on her evening.

With apologies for being a party-pooper, he'd made
his excuses and left. Alone. Insisting that Sarah stay and
enjoy herself.

Because he hadn't wanted her to leave with him. He
hadn't wanted to spend the night with her, either. Even
though he knew it would have been a night of uncom-
plicated fun.

But it would have been with Sarah.

And that wouldn't have been fair to her.

Because it wasn't Sarah his body ached for.

What a disaster. Ten o'clock in the evening, having
been out on a hot date with one of his favourite women,
and the only place he could think of to go was his
brother's house. Because he didn't want to go back to

his own home. And he didn't want to go anywhere else, either.

He was thirty-seven years old, single, tolerably good-looking, very wealthy—and the only people he could think of to spend his time with were his older brother and his wife! His life was falling apart. And he knew exactly who was responsible for it!

He wasn't going to think about her. Refused even to let her image creep into his head.

Which made it doubly difficult to maintain his composure when he walked into Jarrett and Abbie's sitting room a few minutes later, and found Gaye sitting comfortably ensconced in one of the armchairs, Conor cradled snugly in her arms!

As usual, she looked gorgeous! Her hair glowed golden as it lay draped across her shoulders, her eyes were a luminous green, and she had been laughing happily at something Abbie said to her as he walked into the room, giving her a girlish look.

Although, as she turned and saw him standing in the doorway, a guarded expression came over her face.

Which annoyed Jonathan intensely. 'Not interrupting anything, am I?' he snapped harshly.

'Only changing Conor's nappy,' Abbie told him as she stood up gingerly to kiss him lightly on his cheek in greeting, obviously still slightly sore from her operation. 'Unless you would like to do it for me?' she teased as Gaye joined them at the door, a sleeping Conor still cradled in her arms.

'Pass,' Jonathan told her with feeling, looking at Gaye now. 'How are you?' he prompted gruffly.

'Fine, thank you,' she responded. 'My mother is out with Ben again this evening.'

Damn it, she looked fine too—which was more than he looked or felt! 'That's nice,' he acknowledged tightly; Ben really was waging a campaign on Marilyn!

'That's nice?' Jarrett echoed once the two women had left the room. 'As you can see, Abbie took your advice and invited Gaye over to dinner. Whisky?' he enquired, giving Jonathan no chance to make any comment.

'Thanks,' Jonathan accepted. 'And, as I can see, Gaye accepted,' he bit out tautly, still shaken at finding Gaye here in the midst of his family.

'Actually, no.' His brother handed him the glass of whisky. 'She said she couldn't make dinner, either, but she accepted Abbie's suggestion that she pop in and say hello to the baby.'

Why couldn't she make dinner, either? If her mother was out with Ben, what had stopped Gaye going out too?

'I suggest you get used to the idea of seeing her here, Jonathan,' Jarrett continued lightly. 'I have a feeling she and Abbie are going to be great friends!'

Wonderful! Just what he wanted to hear!

'Does Abbie know about Gaye's mother?'

'She didn't,' Jarrett replied. 'But Gaye explained the situation to us both shortly after she arrived. Naturally, I didn't let either of them know that I was already aware of the problem.'

Gaye had just explained the situation to Abbie and Jarrett, whereas he had virtually had to prise the information from her! It was ridiculous to feel angry, he knew it was, and yet that was the emotion he felt. It didn't help that she had seemed so relaxed in Abbie and Jarrett's company when he arrived. She had obviously spent a relaxed and enjoyable evening, whereas he—!

And why hadn't she been able to come to dinner? Nothing to do with Richard Craven, he hoped!

'Thank you for that,' he told his brother distractedly.

'For God's sake sit down, Jonathan,' Jarrett ordered. 'You're making the place look untidy!'

He sat. Not because Jarrett had instructed him to, but because he needed to. It had been quite a shock, finding Gaye here when he'd arrived. Besides, he couldn't leave when he had only just arrived; that would look just too obvious!

He grimaced. 'I suppose Charlie is asleep?'

Jarrett smiled. 'Hours ago. She claims school is boring but she comes home every night exhausted, nonetheless.'

Jonathan smiled too as he thought of his step-niece. Charlie had stolen all the brothers' hearts two years ago, but Jarrett's most of all; he absolutely adored his little stepdaughter.

'I've only called in briefly,' Jonathan said tersely. 'I was a little—offhand with you this afternoon.'

His brother shrugged. 'I don't expect you to be charming all the time, little brother. Besides, I accept that you're under pressure.'

'What?' Jonathan's gaze narrowed suspiciously.

'With my being out of the office most of the time at the moment,' Jarrett explained smoothly. 'I realise that most of the day-to-day running of Hunter's is being left to you and Jordan.'

'Oh.' Jonathan nodded awkwardly.

'What did you think I meant, Jonathan?' his brother prompted.

He willed himself to relax. But he just couldn't, not when he knew Gaye was only upstairs, and she could come back into the room at any moment...

'Jonathan?' Jarrett said again.

What had the two of them been talking about? Oh, yes, the pressure he was under at work. The biggest pressure he had at the moment was that he couldn't stop his attention wandering towards the door as he waited for Gaye to come back into the room!

'I've managed before,' he dismissed, deliberately not answering Jarrett's previous question. Only he knew the emotional pressure he was under. And it was self-inflicted, anyway. A little self-control, and he would be fine again. As long as he didn't accidentally bump into Gaye, as he had tonight, too often!

'I was wondering—' Jarrett broke off whatever he had been about to say as Gaye appeared in the doorway.

She came in quietly, made barely a sound as she stepped softly into the room. But it was as if an alarm bell had gone off inside Jonathan, every muscle and sinew suddenly tense, every nerve-ending crackling with an awareness of her presence.

How to stop this awareness—that was his problem. And how to stop thinking about her!

'Everything okay?' Jarrett smiled at Gaye, a genuinely warm and caring smile.

Jonathan could have hit him for smiling at Gaye in that way. His brother had a wife, a wife he loved very much; he had no right to— He was overreacting, Jonathan realised. Jarrett was being no more than friendly to Gaye, obviously liked, not desired her.

It was simply that it was Gaye he had smiled at...

Gaye returned Jarrett's smile. 'Abbie is just settling Conor down,' she explained wistfully.

'I'll just go and organise some fresh coffee for all of us,' Jarrett announced before leaving the room.

Jonathan barely heard what his brother said, couldn't take his gaze off Gaye as she stood poised for flight just inside the room. As if she was no happier at being left alone with him than he was with her!

Jonathan's mouth tightened. 'How are you?' he enquired abruptly.

'You already asked me that.' She returned his gaze with those cool green eyes. 'I'm well, thank you. You?'

'The same,' he returned flatly. 'And as we're about to be given coffee—' his mouth twisted derisively at Jarrett's arrogance in assuming they wanted coffee '—we may as well both sit down!'

She hesitated. It was only for a fraction of a second. But it was enough for Jonathan to realise he hadn't been mistaken a few moments ago in assuming she was no more eager to spend time in his company than he was in hers!

And that, in complete contradiction of his own decision to avoid her, made him furiously angry!

Okay, so he hadn't behaved too well the other evening when he had almost made love to her on her own sofa, but other than that, what possible reason could she have for not wanting to see him again?

CHAPTER THIRTEEN

As GAYE sat down in one of the armchairs she could feel anger emanating from Jonathan across the room at her.

She hadn't known he would be calling in here this evening!

When Abbie had telephoned her earlier and invited her to dinner, she had come up with all manner of excuses as to why she couldn't come. In the end she had appeased a disappointed Abbie by agreeing to call in for coffee after dinner. But even that had only come after a few carefully worded questions which ascertained that Jonathan would be nowhere near!

She had been hurt the other evening when he didn't ask to see her again, but as the days had passed—long, tedious days!—she had realised it was because he really didn't want to see her again. She had no idea what she had said or done to offend him, but, much as it hurt her not to see him or be with him, she had no intention of running after him, either.

However, his anger towards her now at finding her at his brother's home seemed to imply he thought that was exactly what she was doing!

She drew in a deep breath, unflinchingly meeting that glittering golden gaze. 'I was told you were busy this evening.' Much as she liked Abbie, she would be deeply upset with the other woman if she found out she had deceived her on that point...

'I was.' He sat down. 'But I was on my way home, and on impulse decided to call in.'

So he hadn't been expected...

On his way home? It was barely ten o'clock when he arrived. A little early to be going home, she would have thought—even if he did have another early appointment in the morning!

'I see,' she nodded, not seeing at all. But then, she had given up all hope of understanding Jonathan these last two days...

He had been the one to chase after her, always seeming to be there, unwilling to take no for an answer. But perhaps he was one of those men who, when he had made the conquest, simply lost interest; the chase was more interesting than the capture.

Whatever the reason, Jonathan was no longer in her life. She was slowly coming to terms with that. She knew it was slowly, because a part of her hadn't been able to pass up this opportunity to spend time with some of his family, to see Jarrett Hunter's eyes, so like Jonathan's.

But shortly after her arrival here she had realised it was like a form of torture to be this close to Jonathan and yet not actually with him at all. The last thing she had expected was that he would walk in partway through the evening!

He wasn't pleased to see her here; that much was obvious. But she liked Abbie, found Jarrett so much less formidable on closer acquaintance, enjoyed the lovingly affectionate relationship between husband and wife. Besides, she had been asked to come, had in no way sought the invitation!

'Ben and my mother seem to be getting on very

well—' She broke off as his expression hardened; she seemed to have said the wrong thing again.

Was there a right thing with Jonathan at the moment? She felt as if she was walking on eggshells even trying to make conversation with him!

'Have you heard from Craven since he sent the flowers?'

She frowned. 'Not since he sent the roses to Mummy, no,' she answered slowly.

'That's something, at least,' Jonathan rasped.

As far as she was concerned, it wasn't anything. Richard wasn't important to her, hadn't been for a long time. It was this man she loved, and he no longer wanted anything to do with her...

She hadn't expected, or wanted, to fall in love with anyone, let alone someone like Jonathan. But love him she did, to the point where she felt totally bewildered by his sudden disappearance from her life. The charming, caring man she had come to know had disappeared, and in his place was someone she didn't recognise.

Maybe this was the real Jonathan? No! She refused to accept that explanation. But she knew it was the only one she was going to get...

Thankfully, Jarrett came back into the room with the tray of coffee at that moment, closely followed by Abbie.

An Abbie who gave them both a considering look before her face lit up with its usual warm smile. 'Two visitors in one evening,' she said happily. 'I was beginning to think I had something contagious instead of having just had a baby!' She sat down to pour the coffee.

'Knowing Jarrett, he's been keeping everyone away,'

Jonathan said sardonically. 'You know how protective he can be.'

Abbie turned to give her husband an affectionate smile, the love they shared more than obvious.

Gaye turned away from such openly expressed love, feeling tearful. She hadn't felt like this since the last time she saw Jonathan! He could make her feel so happy, but he also had the power to make her feel totally miserable!

Was love supposed to be like this? Probably—if that love wasn't returned, she thought heavily.

'I'll just drink my coffee—' she accepted the full cup '—and then I really must be going. I'm on duty in the morning.' Now that Jonathan was here she wanted to leave as soon as possible. She couldn't even begin to imagine what Abbie and Jarrett thought of his distant behaviour towards her, in view of his previous determination. Unless they were aware of the reason for his coolness? If they were, it made it all the more necessary for her to leave!

'No need to rush, Gaye,' Jonathan drawled as he watched her gulp down her hot coffee. 'When you're ready to leave I'll drive you home.'

'No!' she burst out. 'Er—there's no need for that,' she added more calmly. 'It's a pleasant evening; I'll enjoy the walk to the Underground.'

'I don't like the idea of you walking anywhere alone at night,' Jonathan replied disapprovingly.

'Gaye's a big girl, Jonathan,' Jarrett put in dryly before Gaye could reply. 'I'm sure she's capable of taking herself home.'

Jonathan glared at his older brother, and as Gaye watched the silent exchange she had a feeling there was something else going on in this conversation than actually appeared on the surface. She had no idea what it was, but she was grateful for Jarrett's intervention; she had no intention of accepting a lift home from Jonathan when he could barely bring himself to even speak to her!

'I certainly am,' she agreed lightly, putting her cup down to stand up, wearing black trousers and a fitted black blouse. 'It's been lovely to see you both again,' she told the married couple with genuine warmth, carefully avoiding looking at Jonathan. Because she wasn't pleased to see him again, not when he was barely civil to her! 'And the baby is adorable.'

Abbie glanced at Jarrett. 'Actually, the baby is one of the reasons we wanted to see you. Only one of the reasons, I hasten to add,' she smiled. 'Jarrett and I would like you to be godmother to Conor. Along with my friend Alison. She has a little boy too. I'm sure the two of you are going to like each other,' she went on with certainty.

Gaye was stunned. A brief glance at Jonathan showed he was as surprised by the request as she was. And not altogether pleased by it, either. Which wasn't surprising; she very much doubted, after his coolness of the last two days, that he wanted her any more closely associated with his family than was absolutely necessary. Her being godmother to his nephew Conor was altogether too close for Jonathan!

'I'm sure your friend Alison is lovely, Abbie, but—'

'Please don't refuse,' the other woman put in quickly. 'Think about it first,' she encouraged.

'We really would like you to accept, Gaye,' Jarrett agreed.

Gaye looked at him anxiously. She had found Jarrett a difficult man to get to know initially, but by the time

Abbie left the clinic she had ceased to be in awe of him, and this evening she had felt quite relaxed in his company. She had no doubt he was formidable as a businessman, but he obviously adored his wife and children. And she couldn't help but feel flattered that the two of them had obviously discussed it and felt she would make a fitting godmother for Conor. Nevertheless—

'Is one allowed to ask who you've chosen as godfathers?' Jonathan put in with dry sarcasm.

Gaye looked at him sharply. Godfathers... Of course! Jarrett was the only Hunter brother who was married, Conor the only male Hunter heir; it was logical to assume Jarrett and Abbie would choose Jonathan and Jordan as the baby's godfathers.

From the scornful expression on Jonathan's face, it was obviously the logical conclusion he had come up with too! And he was most unhappy with the thought of the two of them being godparents to his nephew...!

It hurt. It felt like a knife being thrust into her chest. And then twisted. What had she done to make Jonathan dislike her so much? She couldn't think of a single thing. Except her earlier assumption that, having chased her and effectively caught her, she was no longer of any interest to him.

And that hurt even more...

'No, one isn't!' Jarrett bitingly answered his younger brother, eyes deeply gold in his unhidden anger. 'One waits until one is damn well asked,' he barked harshly. 'If one is asked at all!' he added coldly.

As she had thought, Jonathan and Jordan were to be the godfathers!

Fight the fights that were worth fighting, and give in gracefully over the ones that weren't, her father had told her. She had no wish to be rude to either Abbie or Jarrett, but this one was definitely worth fighting.

'It really is lovely of you to have asked me,' Gaye brightly told the married couple. 'It really is a wonderful compliment. But I'm sure boys have two godfathers, and only one godmother. And your friend Alison seems to fit the bill admirably, so I—'

'Gaye, I realise this idea has been rather thrust on you,' Jarrett put in soothingly, smiling at her reassuringly. 'But we would like you to think about it. The number of godparents Conor has is, I believe, completely up to his parents. We happen to have chosen who we would like to be his two godmothers.' He shot a darkly warning glare at Jonathan.

Gaye looked at the two men, one so arrogantly assured, the younger stubbornly grim. She had no doubt they would have something to say to each other once she had left, and she didn't envy Abbie being an audience to it...

'I promise I will think about it,' she told Jarrett pleasantly before turning to smile at Abbie. 'Thank you for the coffee, and conversation; I've enjoyed myself.' Until Jonathan arrived so unexpectedly... 'I'll call you, Abbie, and maybe when you're a little more mobile we can meet for coffee or lunch some time?'

If possible, she intended making sure that any further contact with this family was made with Abbie alone, that there was no way it could involve Jonathan. Even accidentally. Like this evening.

'Jonathan,' she said abruptly, inclining her head in parting.

'Gaye,' he returned just as tersely, barely glancing at her.

'I'll come with you to the door.' Abbie stood up.

Gaye wished the other woman wouldn't come out with her; she was barely managing to hold back the tears as it was, and that control could slip at any moment.

She held on long enough to say goodbye to Abbie at the door, long enough for her to walk down the driveway and out onto the pavement. But then she cracked, like the breaking of an eggshell, leaving her raw with pain, the tears seeming to burn her cheeks as they fell so hotly.

What had she done to make Jonathan dislike her so much he couldn't even look at her?

CHAPTER FOURTEEN

'HAVE you been taking lessons at how to be a bastard, or does it just come naturally to you?'

Jonathan knew he had behaved badly towards Gaye, had seen that look of bewildered pain in her expressive eyes before she left; he certainly didn't need Jarrett to tell him so!

He returned his brother's censorious gaze. 'Actually, I just imagined I was you,' he returned scathingly.

Jarrett's mouth twitched derisively. 'Very funny! I hope you realise exactly—'

'Well, I hope you're satisfied, Jonathan!' Abbie burst back into the room, eyes blazing deeply purple, at that moment showing no ill-effects from her recent operation, so angry she could think of nothing else, not even her own discomfort in the week since Conor had been born.

God, was it only just over a week ago? Jonathan inwardly groaned. He could barely remember what his life had been like before Gaye's explosion into it; it felt to him as if he had always been this angry and confused, wanting Gaye in his life, to see her, but at the same time shying away from any deeper emotions.

'He doesn't have the look of a satisfied man to me, Abbie,' Jarrett drawled mockingly before bending to kiss his wife lightly on the lips.

'He doesn't look ashamed of himself, either—and he damn well ought to!' Abbie still glared furiously at Jonathan. 'Gaye was our guest, Jonathan, in our home,

160

and she was perfectly happy to be here until you arrived and started—'

'I wouldn't go so far as to say she's happy, darling,' Jarrett interrupted as he sat down, looking up in amusement as Abbie and Jonathan glared at each other now. 'I think Gaye is just better at hiding her true feelings than Jonathan is…'

Jonathan turned to his brother sharply. 'And what the hell is that supposed to mean?' he growled.

His brother wasn't fazed. 'Take a good look at yourself some time, Jon. A really good look. I think you will find exactly what I mean.'

He looked tired; he already knew that. But that was because he seemed to be having trouble sleeping. But other than looking tired he had seen little change in his own reflection.

'Inside yourself, Jonathan,' Jarrett carried on derisively. 'What's happened to the laid-back Mr Charm?' He raised dark brows.

Jonathan sat down again in one of the armchairs. 'He's out to lunch!' he came back.

His brother chuckled. 'I think he's out on a long holiday—and it isn't doing him any good!'

Jonathan sat further back in the chair, resting his head, closing his eyes. 'I know what you're driving at, Jarrett, but you're wrong. I made a mistake,' he said flatly. 'Gaye just isn't my type.'

'You—'

'Tell me, Jonathan,' Jarrett smoothly cut across Abbie's indignant explosion. 'What *is* your type? Because you don't seem to have got on too well with the woman you were with this evening, either!' he added pointedly.

Because he hadn't been in the mood for Sarah's flamboyance, or her equally fun-loving friends, had wanted— God, he didn't know what he wanted! 'I wasn't in a party mood,' he muttered.

'What sort of mood *are* you in?' his brother demanded.

'It certainly isn't a polite one.' Abbie spoke less angrily now, sitting down on the sofa next to her husband. 'I still can't believe the way you talked to Gaye.' She shook her head dazedly.

Thinking back, neither could Jonathan! He was losing it, that was the problem. His life had had structure, maybe not a lot of purpose, but it was structured to suit his needs; he worked hard, and he played hard. This past week he hadn't seemed to be able to concentrate on work, and, as he had already admitted, he wasn't in the mood for playing!

'Next time I see her I'll apologise for my bad temper, okay?' he bit out dismissively.

Abbie looked at him steadily. 'And when will that be?'

'Abbie—'

'Careful, Jonathan,' Jarrett cut in warningly, his gaze glacial.

Jonathan sighed heavily. 'I really don't know when I'm going to see Gaye again, Abbie,' he answered her evenly, heeding his brother's warning. Besides, what purpose would it serve for him to fall out with his family over this?

'What else don't you know, Jonathan?' Jarrett encouraged softly.

He stood up. 'Well, for one thing, I don't know what the hell I'm doing here! I came originally to apologise for not being able to make dinner this evening, but I just seem to have made things worse, not better.' He sighed. 'You were also right earlier, Jarrett; I had no right to comment on your choice of godparents for Conor.'

It had just thrown him when they had asked Gaye to be godmother. He could see years ahead of him where he wouldn't be able to escape seeing Gaye because she was his nephew's godmother. If he didn't see her, maybe he would be able to get his life back in order. Maybe…

'We want you and Jordan to be the godfathers,' Abbie put in gently.

He knew that. It was another reason he had reacted so strongly earlier.

Gaye knew it too…

Maybe if he left now he would be able to catch up with her—

And do what? Exactly what was he going to say to her if he did catch up with her? He could apologise for being rude. Then what? Drive her home. And then…?

Hell, he didn't know! But he did know he felt a heel for the way he had deliberately ignored her the last two days, and even more so for his behaviour this evening.

'And I graciously accept,' he answered Abbie ruefully. 'As, I'm sure, will Jordan. Now I have to go. I— We'll all go out to dinner one evening. The three of us,' he clarified quickly, even as he headed towards the door.

'I'm sure Abbie and I will look forward to that,' Jarrett told him dryly. 'Gaye took the route through the park,' he added. 'In case you're interested,' he went on as Jonathan gave him a look.

'The park?' he echoed harshly. 'She shouldn't be walking through there on her own at this time of night!'

'She's a big girl now—'

'Jarrett,' he interrupted coldly. 'Much as I love you, one of these days I'm going to take that particular phrase—and take great pleasure in ramming it down your throat!' As Jarrett was, metaphorically, doing to him at the moment!

His brother shrugged unconcernedly. 'It's your phrase; you can do what you like with it.'

Jonathan drew in a deeply controlling breath, nodding briefly to Abbie before leaving.

He was still furious when he reached his car, reversing out of the driveway without his usual caution—straight into the side of a passing vehicle!

For several moments after impact he couldn't believe what had just happened, couldn't believe he had been so lacking in his usual attention that he had actually crashed into another car.

But as the driver of the other vehicle, and a worried-looking Jarrett, having heard the sound of the crash inside the house, both converged on his car at the same time he knew he had to believe it. It wasn't just his life that was a mess; he was too!

And, as he stepped out onto the pavement, he could see that the back of his car was, too!

For the next ten minutes, as apologies were made, addresses exchanged, all he could think of was Gaye walking through the park on her own in the darkness. The fact that she would have done it even if he hadn't turned up this evening, and that he wouldn't then have known anything about it, was totally irrelevant to him; she should have known better!

His anger hadn't abated in the least as he sat outside the station near her home and watched her emerge from the brightly lit area—if anything, it had deepened! If he hadn't been thinking about her earlier then he probably wouldn't have crashed into the other car in the first place!

He pushed open the passenger door as she drew level. 'Get in,' he snapped.

She looked startled, bending down to peer into the interior of the car, not looking any happier when she realised it was him. 'What are you doing here?' She frowned at him, obviously ecstatic at seeing him again!

'Sitting on a double yellow line waiting to get booked for illegal parking,' he rejoined impatiently. 'One disaster in an evening is quite enough, thank you. So just get in, will you?'

After the briefest hesitation she did so, but it was obviously reluctantly. 'What happened to the back of your car?' she asked quietly.

'It had an argument with a Range Rover as I left Abbie and Jarrett's house,' he bit out dismissively, driving in the direction of her home. 'The Range Rover won!'

Her eyes widened, but she said nothing, merely sat silently beside him, her hands folded neatly in her lap.

Jonathan glanced over at her, irritated beyond belief at her lack of comment. Why didn't she say something more about his accident?

Jarrett hadn't said anything, either, but the amused look on his face as he stood watching the exchange between Jonathan and the other driver had spoken volumes!

Gaye didn't look amused, but it was hard to tell what she was thinking when she sat beside him so—so placidly.

'I begin my driving lessons next week.'

When she did speak, it was so far removed from what he had expected that, for a moment, he couldn't believe he had heard her correctly. But then he was absolutely certain that he had.

'I telephoned a driving school earlier today and booked a course of lessons,' she added at his continued silence.

He was silent because she had rendered him speechless! Okay, so he had decided that he wasn't going to teach her to drive, after all, but he hadn't expected her to take the decision out of his hands and arrange lessons with someone else!

'I realise you're a very busy man, with a very busy schedule,' she went on reasonably.

He didn't want to be reasoned with! Even if what she said made perfect sense. Even if he had already made that decision himself!

'Jonathan…?' she prompted at his ongoing silence.

'I am listening, Gaye,' he finally ground out, his attention still fixed on the road ahead. 'If that's what you want to do,' he concurred abruptly. 'Considering my accident earlier, it may be as well if someone else taught you!'

'No matter how good we are, Jonathan, we all make mistakes,' she replied.

Exactly what did she mean by that remark? Exactly what it sounded like—or something else?

Luckily—or unluckily; Jonathan wasn't sure which—they had reached her home by this time, making any answer he might have made seem like a waste of time.

He stopped the car, looking up at the unlit house. 'It doesn't look as if Marilyn and Ben are back yet.'

'No,' she agreed lightly. 'Thank you for the lift—'

'I'll come in and sit with you until they get back, if you like.' The words were out before he could process them through his brain. He listened to himself with a sinking feeling in his stomach. He had avoided even seeing her the last couple of days, and now he was deliberately putting himself in a position of being alone with her. And once he was alone with Gaye he knew he would want to kiss her. Hell, if he were honest, he had been wanting to kiss her since the moment he had walked into Abbie and Jarrett's sitting room and seen her again.

Gaye smiled at his suggestion, shaking her head. 'I have no intention of sitting up for my mother. And she wouldn't expect me to.'

She had no intention of asking him in, either! The way he had behaved these last few days, and again this evening, maybe he deserved this coolness from Gaye, but that didn't stop it from rankling.

God, he was behaving, and thinking—when he took the time to think at all!—like an idiot; one moment he couldn't wait to get away from her, and the next he was annoyed because she should feel the same way about him!

'How about inviting me in for a cup of coffee?' he heard himself say.

He was doing it again; his mouth was working without consulting his brain!

Gaye turned from the action of getting out of the car, looking with puzzlement at him. 'Are you sure that's what you want to do?'

What he wanted was to feel normal again, to act normally too. But he was beginning to think this might be what 'normal' was for him from now on. 'Yes,' he replied tensely.

She raised her brows at his obvious aggression, and then she gave a rueful nod of acquiescence before getting out of the car.

Jonathan followed at a slower pace, mentally berating himself. Get a grip, he warned himself. Or Gaye was going to think he was an idiot too. If she didn't already!

She seemed perfectly relaxed with him as she moved about the comfortable kitchen preparing the coffee. Unlike that first day at the clinic, when she had been so unnerved by his presence she had dropped a spoon! She had been very aware of him that day; now she seemed indifferent to him. And, after forcing himself not to come anywhere near her the last two days, he found that indifference extremely annoying.

Gaye put their coffees on the breakfast-bar, making no effort to move to the formality of the sitting room. Jonathan wasn't sure whether that was a positive or a negative thing, whether she felt relaxed enough with him to stay in the kitchen, or whether she was keeping him in here because he had asked to come inside, and hadn't been invited to do so.

In all of his thirty-seven years Jonathan could never remember trying to fathom the motivation of a woman's actions as he did where Gaye was concerned. He had never been interested enough in the past to bother! What—?

'Would you like to tell me what it is I've done to upset you?'

The directness of her softly spoken question totally threw him. Ben was right; she was Abbie all over again, but a less volatile Abbie, Gaye's very quietness more compelling than any show of temper might have been.

He gave her a considering look. 'What makes you think you've done anything?'

She gave a sad smile, sitting up on the bar stool next to his. 'Possibly the way you've been scowling at me since you arrived at Abbie and Jarrett's this evening?'

No mention of the complete silence from him the last two days. Although he couldn't believe she hadn't been aware of it...

He gave a dismissive shrug. 'I wasn't aware of it,' he said evasively.

Gaye sighed, meeting his gaze steadily. 'I don't believe you.'

His eyes widened. She didn't—! 'That's a pretty blunt accusation,' he burst out finally.

'I thought you would have realised by now, Jonathan, I'm a pretty blunt person.'

No one had ever called him a liar before...

Not because he didn't lie; if the occasion merited it, then he was perfectly capable of telling a lie to protect either his family's or his own privacy. Gaye didn't even seem willing to allow him that. Maybe she felt justified; after all, he had moved in on her life like a tornado— and as quickly left again when the going got too tough!

'You haven't done anything to upset me,' he answered. Except for being gorgeous, caring, funny, intelligent—in fact, everything a man could possibly want in one woman. 'I'm aware I haven't seen you for a couple of days, but, as you pointed out earlier, I'm a busy man.' Even as he said those words, as he watched her flinch at his deliberate coldness, he regretted being so cruelly hurtful.

Gaye stood up abruptly, pain warring with anger in the deep green depths of her eyes. 'Then I had better not keep you any longer,' she returned evenly, her whole body rigid as she faced him.

He winced at her chilly tone. This was what he had wanted, but now that he had got it…! 'Gaye—'

'Jonathan, would you please just leave?' She turned away from him, that tension still in her rigidly held shoulders.

He could go, could leave now, and knew that Gaye would never want to set eyes on him again after the way he had just spoken to her. But to never see her again, never hear that tinkling sound of her laughter, never feel the warmth of her passion—! He couldn't do it!

'But I don't want to just leave,' he groaned as he too stood up. 'Gaye, I don't know what's going on in my head any more. One minute I'm determined not to see you, the next I can't seem to stay away from you—'

'Like earlier,' she guessed huskily. 'When you didn't want to see me at Abbie and Jarrett's,' she explained, 'but then half an hour later you were waiting for me to come out of the station.'

'Yes!' he agreed harshly. 'Exactly like that.'

'But you have no idea why you feel that way?' She looked at him hard.

Of course he had an idea! But it was an unacceptable answer. 'None,' he snapped dismissively. 'And until I do I feel it's unfair to inflict my company on you.'

Gaye still looked at him searchingly, seeming to see straight past his words to the confusion beneath. She sighed, giving him a rueful look. 'For one thing you didn't inflict yourself on me. For another, again I don't believe you when you claim not to know why you feel the way you do—'

'Gaye, don't presume to tell me what I do or do not know!' he cut in angrily. God, this woman infuriated him, so much so that he wanted to shake her and kiss her all at the same time! And the latter was guaranteed to stop those disturbing words tumbling from her lips!

She resisted when he drew her into his arms, which only made him all the more angry. At Gaye for pulling away from him. At himself for wanting the curvaceous warmth of her moulded against him…!

She tasted delicious, as sweet as honey, as heady as wine, and Jonathan felt himself once again losing control. He had known desire and passion many times in the past, but always on his own terms, always with a lazy indifference about the relationship. But with Gaye—! He ached for her, to possess her, to feel her naked and trembling in his arms, with the same passion that swept through him every time he touched her.

Her skin felt like velvet to his touch, her hands trailing a path of heat down the length of his spine. Gaye wanted him too! He was sure of it. And just kissing her was no longer enough…

He moved slightly, so that his lips now caressed one creamy cheek. 'I want you, Gaye. I want you very much,' he growled, knowing his body had already told her that.

'And?' she prompted breathlessly.

'Come home with me!' His arms tightened about her. 'Spend the night with me,' he encouraged huskily.

She looked up at him with wide green eyes, her cheeks flushed, those eyes feverishly bright. 'Why, Jonathan?' she breathed raggedly.

He shook his head impatiently. 'I've just told you. I want you—'

'It isn't enough.' She moved away from him.

He felt feverish, his mind in turmoil. He couldn't think straight, only knew the sudden loss of her. She had wanted him too; he knew she had!

'What more do you want from me, Gaye?' he pleaded with frustration.

But as he looked at the haunted disappointment in her eyes he suddenly knew the answer to that...! He drew in a deeply controlling breath, moving abruptly away from her as the heat of passion died, and his head cleared.

'Hearts and flowers aren't for me, Gaye,' he rasped harshly. 'You've known that from the beginning,' he accused hardly. 'I've never made any secret of it.'

'No, you haven't,' she acknowledged sadly, hands tightly clasped together in front of her. 'I think you had better go now, don't you?' she added, her voice trembling.

For a moment, a brief, mind-numbing moment, he wavered. If he left now he knew he would never hold Gaye again, never know the delicious taste of her lips, the warm, scented perfection of her body. But then sanity returned. He valued his freedom above everything. Didn't he...?

'Yes,' he agreed sharply. 'I had better go. I— Goodbye, Gaye.' His expression was dark as he knew that was the last thing he wanted to say to her. Ever.

He had to say goodbye to her!

Didn't he...?

'Goodbye, Jonathan.' She no longer even looked at

him, her gaze focused somewhere on the wall over his shoulder.

He had to go.

But he could still feel the warm pull of her, her beauty holding him immovable. He didn't want to leave her!

But he was going to.

Oh, yes, he was going to.

With one last aching glance at the pale beauty of her face, he turned and left.

And as the door to the house closed behind him he felt a door inside his heart close too...

CHAPTER FIFTEEN

'DARLING, I have no wish to interfere—'

'Then please don't, Mummy,' Gaye advised, attempting a smile to take any harshness away from her words, the two of them busy in the kitchen, clearing away after their evening meal.

'But you've been working so hard these last two weeks,' her mother commented reprovingly.

'We're short-staffed at the clinic,' Gaye excused. 'Annual holiday, sickness, things like that.' Actually she volunteered to do any shifts that were available. If she was working then she didn't have the time to think about Jonathan! 'And with Ben such a regular visitor,' she added teasingly, 'I haven't exactly been leaving you on your own.'

Her mother's cheeks flushed becomingly. 'Ben has been very kind,' she said. 'But we weren't talking about me, darling—'

'Well, we certainly aren't going to talk about me, Mummy,' Gaye returned lightly.

'Gaye—'

'Mummy!' she said sharply. The only way she had survived the desolation of the last two weeks, since Jonathan left her life so abruptly, had been not to think about him. She had thought her life empty before she met him, but she had never known loneliness like this, of a sort that reached right to the very heart of her.

'Whatever you want to say, Mummy,' she added wearily, 'please don't.'

'But I can't simply stand by and see you so unhappy—'

'Mummy—I—really—can't—talk—about—this!' Her voice broke emotionally from the strain. She had been at such pains to keep this at bay for the last two long, lonely weeks. 'I *can't*, Mummy,' she declared brokenly, her hands tightly gripping the kitchen work-top, knowing she was very close to breaking down in tears.

Jonathan had left her because he couldn't love her, wouldn't allow himself to love any woman. And she loved him so much. So very much...

She looked up at her mother's continued silence, gasping at the pain she could see etched into that agelessly beautiful face. Pain...? It was an emotion her mother had refused to accept in her life these last two years...

As she watched, her mother drew in a shuddering breath, moistening dry, peach-glossed lips. 'Gaye, I— I've been very unfair to you the last two years— No, let me finish,' she insisted as Gaye gave her a startled look. 'I'm only now, with Benjamin's help, beginning to realise exactly what a burden you have been carrying alone since—' She broke off, her face pale. 'Gaye, are you in love with Jonathan?'

Gaye opened her mouth to speak, to deny such an admission. But the words wouldn't come out. She could only stare at her mother, mouth open, eyes wide.

Her mother moved, gently placing her hand on Gaye's arm. 'He's a fine man, Gaye.' She spoke huskily. 'I couldn't have wished for anyone better for you. And I know—I know—' She swallowed hard. 'I know your father would have liked him, too,' she finished in a rush.

Would have. Not should. Not will. But the past tense—*would have*!

'Mummy—' She broke off as the doorbell rang, frowning at the harshness of the intrusion. As far as she was aware, they weren't expecting anyone this evening, Ben claiming a prior engagement. And this conversation with her mother was too important to stop now. 'Mummy!' She stopped her mother as she moved to answer the doorbell. 'We still need to talk,' she said firmly. They had been on the verge of a breakthrough for her mother; she was sure they had!

Her mother smiled at her calmly. 'Don't worry, Gaye. I'm not going to conveniently forget we ever started this conversation,' she reassured her before going out into the hallway.

Gaye felt thoroughly confused. She had no idea what had been going on these last two weeks, deliberately buried in her work as she had been, but there was definitely something different about her mother, something wonderfully different. She—

'Look who's called to see us,' her mother announced brightly as she came back into the kitchen.

Gaye knew who it was even before she saw him standing behind her mother, had somehow felt his presence. As she looked at Jonathan's grimly set features, she knew, despite what he might have said to her the last time they met, that he too had suffered during the last two weeks spent apart.

But what was he doing here now? From his expression, it wasn't a social visit!

'Good evening, Jonathan,' she greeted coolly, pleased that she managed to sound so composed.

Because inside she was doing a rapid inventory of her

appearance! She had changed into comfortable jeans and loose top when she came in from work an hour ago; the fact that she and her mother were eating alone this evening meant that she hadn't had to dress for dinner. She wished now that she had taken a bit more trouble with her appearance, her face bare of make-up, her hair loose about her shoulders. But how could she possibly have guessed that Jonathan would arrive so unexpectedly?

'Gaye,' he responded curtly, continuing to look at her broodingly.

'If the two of you will excuse me?' her mother put in graciously. 'There are some things I need to do upstairs.'

Gaye very much doubted that, especially as the two of them had decided over their meal that they would probably have a game of chess after dinner. Not that she could exactly blame her mother for wanting to get away from the tension emanating out of Jonathan, so strong it could be physically felt.

What on earth was wrong with him? She hadn't seen him for two weeks, hadn't ever expected to see him again, and now that he was here all he could do was glower at her from beneath frowning brows!

'Can I get you something to drink?' Gaye offered once they were alone. 'Tea? Coffee?'

'A glass of that will be fine,' he grated, nodding in the direction of the red wine they had opened earlier to accompany their meal; even if the supper was informal, her mother liked to observe the niceties.

Gaye got him a glass and poured some of the wine, still unsure of exactly what Jonathan was doing here. Whatever the reason, he looked far from happy about it!

'Is everything all right? Your family are well?' she enquired politely, although she knew Abbie, Jarrett and

the two children were all fine, had met Abbie for coffee
only yesterday. And she was sure the other woman
would have mentioned it if there were any worries with
Jonathan and Jordan. But Abbie hadn't mentioned either
brother. At the time Gaye had been grateful for the omis-
sion, couldn't even talk about Jonathan without becoming emotional. But now she wasn't so sure; it would
have been better if Abbie had told her if something was
wrong.

'They're fine. I'm fine,' he replied carelessly. 'I'm not
here to talk about me! Or my family,' he added grimly,
drinking down half the wine in his glass with one gulp.

Gaye eyed him warily. 'Do you want to stay in here,
or would you rather move through to the sitting room?'

His eyes narrowed. 'Why?'

She shrugged. 'I just thought—'

'I'm fine right here.' And to emphasise the point he
sat down on one of the two bar stools.

He was less imposing sitting than he had been when
he was standing, but even so his personality was so
forceful it didn't really make that much difference!

'Ben called round to see me this evening,' he said
without delay, his gaze still narrowed on her.

So Jonathan had been Ben's prior engagement. Well,
she couldn't see anything strange in that; the two men
were friends, after all.

She still stood, leaning back against one of the kitchen
units. And she still eyed Jonathan warily. 'Ben seems to
be getting through to my mother.' She warmly remembered her earlier conversation with her mother—and
quite a lot of hope. 'I really think—'

'He told me that he feels he's very close to the barrier

coming down completely. That means you'll be free to lead your own life again,' he said caustically.

She hadn't quite thought of it in those terms, had just been pleased that Ben's work with her mother over the last two weeks seemed to be working. She also felt a little guilty that she had been so caught up in her own problems the last two weeks that she hadn't even noticed the change in her mother!

'I suppose it does,' she said slowly.

Jonathan's mouth twisted. 'Ben also told me that he met Richard Craven here the other evening.'

Ben seemed to have told Jonathan rather a lot of things! And from the grimness of Jonathan's expression this last revelation hadn't pleased him at all.

But Ben hadn't been altogether truthful about his having met Richard; the two men had only met briefly on the doorstep, having arrived at the same time. Ben had been admitted. Richard had not. After leaving the two women alone for almost two weeks, Richard had changed his mind again and had decided to have another try at persuading her mother to act under his direction. Gaye hadn't been surprised by this second attempt, knew him too well to believe in the sincerity of that message he had put on the card that had arrived with his flowers. But this time Gaye had left him in no doubt as to how her mother felt about working with him!

But it was curious that Ben had mentioned that brief meeting with the other man to Jonathan at all... And there was also that conversation with her mother earlier... What were her mother and Ben up to? Because Gaye suddenly had a feeling they were up to something!

'Jonathan, I think that you and I—'

'Exactly—you and I!' he echoed forcefully. 'If you

think I'm going to allow Richard Craven to charm his way back into your life after what he did to you—! I'll break his damned neck first! I've already warned him off once,' he continued fiercely. 'Obviously I didn't make myself clear enough—'

'You—warned—Richard—off?' Gaye repeated incredulously. 'Exactly when did you do a thing like that?' And why?

'I had been to see him the day before he sent your mother those flowers,' Jonathan snapped. 'If they were for your mother!'

She remembered now how strangely he had reacted to the roses when he'd arrived that evening...

'They *were* for my mother, Jonathan,' she insisted quietly. 'And I'm more concerned with why you felt it necessary to go and see Richard...' She gave him a thoughtful look.

Jonathan stood up restlessly, tension oozing out of him. 'So that you didn't get hurt again. The man isn't fit to be in the same room as you, let alone— He doesn't deserve you, Gaye,' he bit out harshly.

'Surely that's for me to decide?' she rejoined softly, hope—desperate, yearning hope—starting to well up inside her.

He shook his head. 'You're too emotional at the moment to think rationally. One minute you're laughing, the next you're close to tears. It isn't possible to make life-changing decisions under those circumstances,' he told her arrogantly.

'The same could be said of someone who is charming and caring one moment, and then becomes distant and abrupt the next,' she pointed out.

'You're talking about me?'

Her mouth quirked at his indignant tone. 'Does it sound like you? Jonathan, what I was going to say a few minutes ago was that I think my mother and Ben are playing matchmakers!' She sighed. 'I have no interest in Richard, wouldn't even let him into the house, despite what Ben may have told you about the other evening. And earlier my mother was trying to find out how I felt about you. Separately, perhaps the two things don't mean anything, but when you consider my mother and Ben's closeness now, and you put the two conversations together—! Jonathan, I believe we've been set up,' she declared.

His eyes were narrowed. 'For what purpose?'

She looked at him. She could say that her mother and Ben knew how miserable she had been the last two weeks, that the older couple had decided the two of them belonged together. Or she could claim not to know why they were doing it. But to choose the latter course, after the last two weeks of misery, was unthinkable!

She moistened her lips before speaking. 'You're right about one thing, Jonathan—I am very emotional at the moment. But there is a reason for that—'

'Of course there's a reason for it.' He grasped her arms, shaking her slightly. 'This situation with your mother is coming to a climax; it's sure to be unsettling for you. But you have to give yourself time. You can't possibly know how you feel about Richard Craven under these circumstances.'

Richard again... 'I've already told you how I feel about Richard; I'm simply not interested. And never will be,' she stated firmly. 'However—'

'There isn't a 'however', Gaye,' Jonathan broke in harshly.

'Oh, but there is,' she insisted determinedly; now that
she had made her mind up, she intended having her say.
'I'm not in love with Richard, doubt that I ever was. But
I am in love.'

Even as she said the words she felt a sinking feeling
in her stomach. This wasn't right. She couldn't possibly
calmly stand here and tell Jonathan it was him she loved!

But why couldn't she? Could it make the situation
between them any more unbearable than it already was?
The answer to that had to be no! And he was jealous of
Richard; she was sure of it...

Jonathan's fingers tightened on her arms. 'Who is he?'
he ground out. 'Tell me who he is and I'll—'

'He's a wonderful man,' she told him, hope bursting
free inside her. Jonathan was jealous; she knew he was!
'Very caring. Very handsome—'

'Looks aren't everything, Gaye,' he rasped. 'Craven
should have more than shown you that!'

'Oh, the man I love isn't narcissistically good-
looking,' she assured him. 'Far from it. In fact,' she
added mischievously, 'sometimes his mood can be decidedly unattractive!'

Jonathan looked triumphant at the admission. 'Well,
doesn't that tell you that perhaps you're making a mistake about this man too?' He pounced with satisfaction.
'You're too beautiful, too loving and caring yourself to
settle for anything less in return.'

'Oh, I'm not going to settle for second-best,
Jonathan,' she told him, her own certainty about his feelings for her growing by the minute. The hard part was
going to be to get him to admit them!

Some of his triumph faded. 'Does this man love you
in return?' he said flatly.

'I think so.' She smiled, her eyes, she was sure, glowing with love for him. 'It's just a question of getting him to say the words!'

'You mean he hasn't even told you—! Gaye, what the hell sort of man is he that he won't even *tell* you how he feels about you?' he said exasperatedly.

She shrugged. 'He's a man who doesn't trust love. A man who grew up with a mother who taught him all too well that it wasn't wise to love any woman.' She steadily met his gaze after making these pronouncements.

Jonathan became very still, opening his mouth to speak, and then closing it again without saying a word. And then opening it again. And closing it again in silence.

Gaye's smile turned to an indulgent laugh. 'This must be a first—Jonathan Hunter lost for words!'

He shook his head dazedly. 'Only the right ones,' he said gruffly. 'Gaye, I—I—'

'It doesn't matter, Jonathan.' She moved towards him, her arms about his waist as she rested her head against his chest. 'I can say it for both of us.' She looked up at him. 'I love you very much, Jonathan. So very, very much,' she added emotionally.

He swallowed hard. 'Enough to marry me?'

That hope in her heart blossomed to uncontainable proportions, tears filling her eyes, her throat moving convulsively. 'Enough *not* to marry you, if that's the way you want things to be,' she admitted chokily.

'Oh, no.' His arms moved about her possessively. 'I've behaved like a damned fool these last two weeks, Gaye. I tried to convince myself that I could live without you in my life. What an idiot! I've been so miserable my friends don't want to be near me, my family is giving me a wide berth, and my secretary of the last ten years is threatening to resign if I don't lighten up!' He put his hand beneath her chin, tilting her face up to his. 'I love you very much, Gaye Royal,' he told her shakily. 'I want to marry you, and keep you with me for ever.'

'For ever sounds ideal to me, my darling Jonathan,' she said breathlessly just before their lips met.

She had it all now. Jonathan. His love. Their future together. She only hoped for ever was long enough!

CHAPTER SIXTEEN

'IF I WASN'T absolutely positive that some time in the near future Ben's going to be my father-in-law,' Jonathan muttered at Gaye's side, 'I would be tempted to go over there and wipe off that smile he has on his face every time he looks at me!'

Gaye laughed huskily, glancing down the room where they were holding their wedding reception at the man who sat so protectively at her mother's side.

The wedding of Gaye Royal, daughter of Marilyn Palmer and the late Terence Royal, to the extremely eligible Jonathan Hunter had attracted more than its fair share of publicity; there had been dozens of reporters outside the church earlier today, both before the service and when they'd emerged out into the sunshine as husband and wife. But through it all Ben had kept the reporters away from Marilyn, and the door had been firmly closed on their private reception to prevent any further intrusion into what was, after all, a family affair.

Her mother was bearing up very well under the barrage of publicity that had followed the wedding announcement, and since their talk together Marilyn's recovery seemed to be happening in leaps and bounds. So much so that Gaye shared Jonathan's view that Ben would become his father-in-law some time in the future...

'I think, my darling—' Gaye looked laughingly up at her husband '—that you may be kept rather busy if you decided to take that particular action! Jarrett has the same smile, as do several of your friends. And Jordan just looks totally disgusted.' She glanced down the table at her brother-in-law. 'I think he feels totally betrayed by both you and Jarrett!'

Jonathan looked over to where his brother sat. 'He doesn't look too happy, does he?' he acknowledged laughingly.

Gaye shook her head. 'I feel quite sorry for the young lady he brought with him.'

Jonathan gave the redhead seated at Jordan's side a considering look, shrugging as he turned back to Gaye. 'She looks as if she can take care of herself,' he pronounced.

She did indeed, Gaye decided after watching the other woman for several seconds.

'Hey.' Jonathan drew her attention back to him, lifting her hand to kiss the plain gold ring he had placed there earlier in the day. 'I love you, Mrs Hunter,' he told her happily.

'I love you too, my darling Mr Hunter.' She touched his cheek gently, love shining out of the green depths of her eyes. 'For ever and always.'

He nodded. 'I won't settle for anything less.'

Neither would she. Not for a minute, or a second less.

If you enjoyed what you just read,
then we've got an offer you can't resist!

Take 2 bestselling love stories FREE!

Plus get a FREE surprise gift!

Coming Next Month

HARLEQUIN PRESENTS®

THE BEST HAS JUST GOTTEN BETTER!

#2049 MISTRESS BY ARRANGEMENT Helen Bianchin
(Presents Passion)
Michelle is stunned when wealthy businessman
Nikos Alessandros asks her to be his social companion for a
few weeks. Will Michelle, under pressure from her family to
make a suitable marriage, find herself becoming a mistress
by arrangement?

#2050 HAVING LEO'S CHILD Emma Darcy
(Expecting!)
Leo insisted she marry him for the sake of their unborn child.
But despite his fiery kisses, Teri couldn't forget that Leo had
never considered marrying her before she got pregnant.
Could they turn great sex into eternal love?

#2051 TO BE A BRIDEGROOM Carole Mortimer
(Bachelor Brothers)
Jordan is the youngest Hunter brother. His devilish good
looks have helped him seduce any woman he's ever wanted—
except Stazy. There's only one way for Jordan to get to the
head of Stazy's queue—become a bridegroom!

#2052 A HUSBAND OF CONVENIENCE Jacqueline Baird
When an accident left Josie with amnesia, she assumed that
her gorgeous husband, Conan, was the father of her unborn
baby. They shared passionate nights until she remembered
that theirs was actually a marriage of convenience....

#2053 WEDDING-NIGHT BABY Kim Lawrence
Georgina decided she couldn't attend her ex-fiancé's wedding alone—she needed an escort! Callum Stewart was
perfect: gorgeous, dynamic...and on the night of the
wedding he became the father of her child!

#2054 THE IMPATIENT GROOM Sara Wood
(Society Weddings)
Prince Rozzano di Barsini whisked Sophia Charlton away to
Venice in his private jet. One whirlwind seduction later, she'd
agreed to be his bride. But why was Rozzano in such a hurry
to marry? Because he needed an heir...?